THE LAST
INDIAN
AND LIZZIE

Stephen Adams

ORIGINAL WRITING

© 2011 Stephen Adams

All rights reserved. No part of this publication may be reproduced in any form or by any means—graphic, electronic or mechanical, including photocopying, recording, taping or information storage and retrieval systems—without the prior written permission of the author.

978-1-908282-88-0

A CIP catalogue for this book is available from the National Library.

Published by ORIGINAL WRITING LTD., Dublin, 2011.

Printed by CAHILL PRINTERS LIMITED, Dublin.

Contents

Foreword ix

Chapter One
SOUTH LONDON - 1947 1

Chapter Two
THE VIRGIN ISLANDS - 2000 3

Chapter Three
CARIBBEAN 17

Chapter Four
SOUTH LONDON - 1947 20

Chapter Five
SOUTH LONDON 23

Chapter Six
COUNTY WEXFORD, IRELAND - LATE 1930S 36

Chapter Seven
COUNTY WEXFORD - 1920'S 40

Chapter Eight
TIMELINE - COUNTY WEXFORD   44

Chapter Nine
DISASTER - COUNTY WEXFORD EARLY 1940S   50

Chapter Ten
SUNDERED FAMILY - COUNTY WEXFORD   55

Chapter Eleven
INCARCERATION - COUNTY WEXFORD   64

Chapter Twelve
LIZZIE'S LOST CHILDHOOD   69

Chapter Thirteen
RELEASED INTO THE WORLD   72

Chapter Fourteen
SOUTH LONDON - 1950S   75

Chapter Fifteen
COMING TOGETHER   77

Chapter Sixteen
CARIBBEAN – PRESENT DAY   87

Chapter Seventeen
INDIA - 1947   91

Chapter Eighteen
INDIA - 1840S … 103

Chapter Nineteen
FAMILY TREE … 107

Chapter Twenty
INDIA - 1870S … 116

Chapter Twenty One
RANDHAWA SINGH … 120

Chapter Twenty Two
THE ANGLO / INDIAN UNION … 124

Chapter Twenty Three
THE FIRST ANGLO INDIANS … 126

Chapter Twenty Four
JO'S STORY … 129

Chapter Twenty Five
JO IN DARJEELING … 135

Chapter Twenty Six
HIMALAYAN BOARDING SCHOOL … 137

Chapter Twenty Seven
JO IN LOVE … 141

Chapter Twenty Eight
ERIC AND JO'S WEDDING   147

Chapter Twenty Nine
INDIA 14TH FEBRUARY 1938   151

Chapter Thirty
FRENCH SOJOURN - 1958   153

Chapter Thirty One
IRELAND - 1959   163

Chapter Thirty Two
LIZZIE AND ME   168

Chapter Thirty Three
LONDON - 1960 TO 1963   177

Chapter Thirty Four
IRELAND - 1963 TO 1970   186

Chapter Thirty Five
CARIBBEAN   189

Chapter Thirty Six
NOWADAYS AND REFLECTIONS 1   195

Chapter Thirty Seven
NOWADAYS AND REFLECTIONS PART 2   198

Chapter Thirty Eight
OCTOBER 2009 202

Chapter Thirty Nine
TWIN SHOCKS 207

Chapter Fourty
THE ENDGAME 212

Foreword

A boy is born in North Eastern India in 1938. He is the second son of Anglo Indian parents. They live as their earlier generations have, in a community of Anglo Indians created by the East Indian Railway Company. Their lives are happy, stable and they enjoy a comfortable lifestyle. The story tracks the boy's ancestry down his mother's maternal line, for five generations. An Englishman and his new wife emigrated to Colonial India in the 1870's. The story tells of how he eventually fathered a family of Anglo Indians. This is followed through the generations and describes typical Anglo Indian life in the railway communities of the Raj.

In the same year a girl is born to a couple in rural County Wexford, Ireland. She is the fourth surviving daughter. A boy born before her didn't survive his first year. The family live in a small rented cottage. It is a young family, who like many all over rural Ireland, have a hard, but happy family life. Electricity, running water and main drainage are still decades away. Her parents and close relatives have always lived in their immediate neighbourhood. The men have traditionally worked as farm labourers. The life and times of rural Ireland and the extreme hardships many people faced in those days has been very well documented elsewhere. No attempt is made to explore that here. However, when the girl is nearly six years of age an event takes place that devastates her life and that of the entire family, forever.

The lifestyle and environment of these two families are vastly different and in very different parts of the world. This is a narrative about these two people. It tracks their lives from birth to their late teens and beyond. The story also explores their ancestry back several generations.

The Anglo Indian race started as far back as the early seventeenth century. All the European Colonists were battling each other to claim territory, wealth and power in India and the East Indies. Many of these traders fathered children with Indian women, and mixed race people were the result. As time went on and the British presence in India developed, the Anglo Indian population grew. The book develops this story in more detail.

A little known sociological fact is the destruction of the Anglo Indian race. It ended in 1947, when India became independent. Being neither Indian, nor British, the future looked bleak for them. The Anglo Indians who remained in India will gradually be assimilated by the indiginous population and the majority who left India are being assimilated all over the world.

The two storylines play out separately until fate or chance brings the two face to face.

The telling of this tale is also a little unusual. The time line moves to the millennium. Our Anglo Indian is on a sailing trip in the Caribbean with his best friend. They have been friends for thirty five years and he has been promised this story since they met. Time and life have always put off the telling, but now they have all the time.

Chapter One

SOUTH LONDON - 1947

"Dogseeeeey!" the shrill call cut through yellow brown smog. The old green iron footbridge that crossed rail sidings which led to the shunting yard, was lined on both sides by awestruck five to 12 year olds.

The riveted plates and struts were still rimed with frost, despite it being dusk on this late November afternoon. This was South London in 1948 and everyone choked on the murk that passed for air.

Not far away an old black and rusting steam locomotive was pumping its load into the grime as it shunted coal wagons to the yard. On the bridge, lines of mouths, all facing in the same direction, mimicked the shunter with little puffs of breath.

The bridge had two flights of steps separated by a half landing at each end. The steel decking of the bridge was 16 feet above the tracks and about 25 feet long. Dogsy stood at one end of this, his eyes twitched between the end of the 25 foot runway and at his audience lining each side of the parapets.

A few brave kids would make the jump, but only as far as the half landing and a safe platform. With our hearts hammering, we waited. This was bloodlust and Dogsy knew it. A certain kind of madness coursed through him.

While the rest of us were members of groups, he was a loner and totally without fear.

A lone foot started stamping the steel and was immediately picked up. Chanting developed as I watched, entranced. His face tightened around the eyes and mouth, and he started rocking from heel to toe on both canvas plimsole shod feet.

As he sprang forward, the little puffs of breath stopped, as did the chanting. We gaped at the figure in total silence and awe. The only sound was his plimsoles pounding the steel decking. It was as if this was a dream and was taking place in slow motion.

His right foot hit the end of the deck above the top step at full speed, and he launched himself forward. Crouching like a cat and focused at the base of the steps, there was nothing between him and success...or the hospital.

How I wanted to see his mind as he hung in the air for what seemed like an eternity. Did he know what to expect when gravity wrenched him down, crunching on to those waiting steps? Galleries of eyes on each side gaped as he flew past and down until, incredibly, he bounced off the fourth step from the bottom and rolled like a ball to the ground.

He turned over on to his back, with a toothy grin that said, "Beat that". The little puffs of breath started again.

Chapter Two

THE VIRGIN ISLANDS – 2000

Fifty odd years on and I reach back to the recesses of memory. Back as far as my mind will allow. However, it's difficult to be organised about it. Random cameos and childhood images flash by and dim. Almost impossible to create a pattern or continuity, but desire keeps the reverie alive. Thoughts of Dogsy and London smog half a century ago, tripped easily from my mind as we crept between Virgin Gorda and Mosquito Island.

The keel slid through water, inches above the sandy bottom, as the engine pulled us gently through. What wind there was came from the rear starboard quarter and took the edge off the late morning sun. Up ahead the pale turquoise water darkened as the sandy spit between the islands fell away to deeper water.

The burr of the engine through the teak fore deck, induced slumber and caused my mind to daydream. What in God's name switched my mind back so far in time and to a situation so far removed from the Caribbean amazed me, and the experience was so vivid that I wanted more, but the moment had passed for the time being anyway. I knew that we would be busy getting under way shortly, so I lay on my back to savour the moment.

A lone frigate bird hovered overhead, its black silhouette etched against the cobalt, blue sky. Jack had made this passage many times in Christo and showed no anxiety. Only if there was a swell might there be a problem. But still he concentrated on the depth gauge, until we reached deeper water. I went back to the cockpit to look at the depth reading.

"Nerves of steel, eh? Ha! By the way, have you made a decision about the fresh water pump because the job we did won't last long," I asked.

"I know and we can't risk being without it after tomorrow. I radioed Sam while you were nodding and he can get a replacement this afternoon, so I think that we'll head to Cruz Bay now and do it," Jack responded.

The sea bed fell away before us and the water colour confirmed it.

"Take the helm, Ads, and I'll get some sail up," Jack said. We had a gentle 12 knots of wind from astern, so I knew we should make Cruz Bay by around three. Virgin Gorda slid by on the port side as Jack winched the main up, and then unreefed the Genoa. There was enough wind to fill the sails so he cut the motor, and we got the mizzen up too. He went below for a few minutes and emerged with a couple of beers.

"Thanks, Jack, I must have died and gone to heaven!" He grinned. I had flown in to Tortola two days before on the shuttle from San Juan. The twin turboprop Fokker flew slow enough to take in the scenery and to enjoy the beauty of the Caribbean Sea, ranging in colours from deep blue to the palest turquoise as reefs and beaches intruded. Landscapes contrasted starkly with the pervading greens of Ireland. White coral beaches, lined with sea grape and palms faded into dry red soil and low scrub, which was typical of these islands. Absorbed in the view from my window seat and thinking in anticipation of stepping from the plane into 28 degrees of tropical sunshine, I did not at first hear the comment from the person beside me.

"You on holiday?"

I turned to face someone who obviously was not. "Yeah, for a month."

"Charter?"

"No, my friend has a ketch here in Tortola." His Cockney accent came out of a mouth with a lot of teeth missing. The face of a man in his late 40s and one which had become very used to the climate and north east trade winds of the Caribbean, topped with a head of scant bleached hair.

"What's his name?" he asked.

I looked at him and said, "Bet you know a few people around here. His name is Jack Collins." I noticed a slightly puzzled look on his face before he said,

"Yeah, I know Jack but he had a berth in Cruz Bay in the USVI the last time I met him. I'm a marine tech and I did a few jobs for him last year."

"Oh, that's right," I replied. "He shifted here just before the hurricane season and had the fuel tank scoured in Roadtown. Had to sort out a recurring fuel pump blockage."

The airport was at the eastern end of the island and was designed for light aircraft up to the size of the Fokker. We were descending now with Tortola on the starboard side.

"As I recall the boat is called, "Christo", isn't it?" he asked.

I nodded and replied, "Two of his sons may be joining us in a couple of days."

I could feel the thrum of the turboprops through the seat. The plane banked steeply as the pilot adjusted for the glide path and I looked down at scrub and a narrow dirt track, leading down to a stony shore and glittering water. We were low enough to disturb a couple of pelicans who lifted off a small jetty, and flew away from the plane.

As I stepped from the air conditioned aircraft on to the tarmac, it was as if I had arrived on a different planet. I turned to my companion with a grin on my face and offered my hand, "Stephen Adams or 'Ads' to my friends." He gripped my hand.

"Jim Bowman, good to meet you. Have a good holiday." We walked to the terminal building and the waiting customs officers.

A black officer quizzed Jim as I walked

through and there was Jack in a polo shirt, shorts, a baseball cap and a broad grin.

"Hi, you old reprobate. I hope there's plenty of ice on board for the Vodka." We hugged as always and back slapped.

"Don't worry, my first priority on board is the refrigeration. Without that, we aren't going anywhere!"

I was a day late due to a pilot's dispute; I had been routed through Philadelphia and had overnighted there. There was a foot of hardened snow and it was five below. I was now standing in 28 degrees.

"Sorry for the delay but I can tell you that Philadelphia was no consolation for this. I guess it's my loss." All I had was a canvas bag over my shoulder as we walked away from the terminal. The tarmac had a film of fine sand on it and the breeze would sometimes create small eddies.

"Christo is at anchor in the bay just up the road, but let's have a beer at the Cay Bar first," said Jack.

The sound of a car coming behind us forced us to vacate the centre of the road. As it slowed alongside, Jim said,

"Yo, Jack, how're ya doing? I heard you had moved to this neck of the woods!" Jim's leathery face beamed out of the front passenger window.

"Hi, Jim, good to see you, too." The two shook hands. Jack asked, "Where are you heading, Jim?"

"I'm going to Roadtown to pick up a charter. I've contracted to skipper it for some Yanks. I have to pick 'em up on St Thomas in a couple of days. They've got it for three weeks and I haven't got a clue what they're like," he sighed.

"Well, we may be close enough in a few days time so keep your eyes peeled for Christo, but strictly only if you have eligible babes on board," countered Jack with a grin.

As the cab lurched forward, Jim shouted, "See you guys around."

"Not if I see you first," muttered Jack. The bay opened up in front of us as we walked around a bend in the road.

It was littered with yachts at anchor or on moorings. A wooden jetty to our left had a number of dinghies and tenders tied up. A white sandy beach followed the tarmac road ahead of us. We walked on to the Cay Bar up to our right.

"Hi Maisie," Jack called to the middle aged, plump woman behind the bar.

"What'll it be, Jack?" replied the grouchy woman.

"Two cold beers," I said.

"She must have had a row with her old man; she's normally good fun," said Jack.

"Hey, Maisie, who rattled your cage this morning?" This came from a fat, red-faced man at the other end of the bar, followed by a nicotine-croaked guffaw.

"Go fuck yourself, Paxman!" countered a belligerent Maisie.

Jack smiled, "Usual light banter."

"What's the plan for today, Jack?" I asked as we finished our beers.

"We'll head straight for Leverick Bay now and find a berth for the night. I want to get some provisions there as well. How does that sound?" he answered.

"Jack, as far as I'm concerned, I'm in heaven. You make the decisions and give the orders. I really don't care. I'm going to just lap it all up."

"Look, Ads, there's not going to be any crap here. We're just going to have some fun, right?"

I flipped off his cap as I got up, "Ok," I laughed. We walked straight across the road to the beach and over to a new 10 foot gullwing semi-inflatable dinghy, with a 10 hp Yamaha on the stern. "You'd better get those shoes off now before they get wet. You won't be needing them again for a month," Jack advised.

The sun glittered on a flat sea as I looked across the bay at the tethered yachts. A lone Pelican sat perched on a stump at the end of the jetty, preening himself. We shoved off and stepped into the boat.

The two stroke strummed into life immediately and pushed us gently out towards Christo, each of us alone with our thoughts for the moment. I wondered did he ever get used to this life or was it still a kick each time he did this? Christo was only his for the last two years and he had sailed it down to the Caribbean from Connecticut, where he had bought it. But he had been spending nearly half his time here in the British Virgin Islands for a dozen years or more. Christo was his third yacht.

We were in no more than 10 feet of crystal water and I looked down at a dappled sandy bottom. As we approached Christo, I wanted to gape at her for the first time.

"Circle her, Jack; I want to have a good look."

He turned the Yamaha so that we would go around at about 60 feet out.

"She was designed and built on the Solent, Ads, only one of six. You can tell from her lines that she's a cruiser, not an out and out racer."

I admired the graceful lines and the quality of finish and fittings. The hull and superstructure were white GRP. The main and mizen masts and booms were anodised aluminium and rigging in stainless steel. As we came round from the bow to the stern, I could see the beautifully proportioned transom with stainless steel ladder and "CHRISTO "in black edged gold.

Jack brought the dinghy alongside the stern and I grabbed the ladder with the dinghy painter in my other hand.

"Get on board, Ads, and tie the painter to the stern cleat. I'll pass up the gear."

The spacious cockpit was a full 12 feet long with seating and lockers on each side and at the back. In front of the rear lockers was the binnacle with compass and a great mahogany rimmed stainless steel wheel.

"Go on down, Ads, and take the cabin, first on right. If the boys arrive they can share the forward cabin. I'm afraid that the fresh water pump is acting up so you can't shower, but I'll get around to it before the day is out," Jack said that as he chucked my bag to me. While I was changing and stowing my gear, I could hear an outboard engine approaching and then coming alongside.

"Hi, Gus, Pam, good to see you. What brings you over here?" called Jack.

"Hi Jack. I may well ask you the same," countered Gus as he threw Jack the dinghy line, "I could murder a beer."

I could hear them coming aboard.

"Here to pick up some friends from Pittsburg. Over for a week's vacation," said Pam.

"Snap," said Jack as I emerged from down below. "Let me introduce you to my best friend, Stephen Adams who arrived on the last shuttle." Gus was a wiry, slightly stooped man around 60 with a moustache like Groucho Marx but like Jack, looked fit and used to an active life. He had a firm handshake to go with a toothy grin.

"How'd you get tanned so quick since you just arrived?" he asked.

"Well it's permanent and a long story, but I'm looking forward to topping it up," I laughed.

Pam was a poker-faced woman of around 45 and I guessed a little eccentric. She had a gamey eye on me as she sipped at the can.

"I should warn you that Pam looks at every half decent looking newcomer as a possible conquest," Gus said as she shot a sharp look in his direction. I imagined that this was normal and intended to defuse any flirting.

"You planning any blue water sailing?" asked Jack.

"No, a week is not long enough for that but in any case, this pair is not really that interested in sailing. So I think that it will be a little Island hopping and a lot of partying!"

"How about you?" asked Pam.

"We haven't had a chance to discuss all that in detail but we hope to get down to Trinidad, after clearing up a few outstanding jobs on the boat," said Jack.

"Gus, honey, I think these boys need a woman's touch on a trip like that. You know, a bit of cooking, cleaning, and whatever. You can do without me for a couple of weeks, couldn't you?" Pam's honey tones drew the expected response from Gus. A withering look from Gus answered her question. Jack put his arm around Pam and commiserated.

"Never mind, Pam, it's our loss and I guess we'll just have to get on without you." We all laughed. After another half hour of banter, they took their leave and we released the mooring.

"It's like that around here, Ads, people just dipping in and out of each other's lives and not getting in any way involved with each other. That suits me fine. Columbus named the island Virgin Gorda (fat Virgin) after that hill," Jack explained as we came into Leverick Bay. He pointed to a mooring buoy 300 metres ahead and said, "Go forward and pick up that mooring, Ads. I don't think we'll get one closer in."

On the way in we had passed a French cruise ship at anchor on our port side. There were people in single sail multicolour dinghies having fun, obviously from the cruise ship.

"It should be lively on shore tonight, Ads, but before we relax, we have some chores to do."

It took us an hour and a half to take the fresh water pump apart, clean it and the filter, and put it all back, but it really needed replacing. We spent another hour on spit and polish, before Jack was happy enough to throw off his T shirt, and dive off the stern. Before he had time to surface, I was in after him.

The layer of sweat and grime I had built up sloughed off, and the sharp edge of diving into northern seas was not there. When I surfaced, Jack was swimming strongly away from the boat. I turned on to my back and swam slowly around Christo.

The sun was getting low as we sat refreshed and enjoyed a second vodka and soda with plenty of ice.

"It seems a long time ago since I left San Juan, but it was only this morning and the night is young. I'm looking forward to some of the fabled seafood tonight, Jack, so I hope you know a good place where we can do that and enjoy a beer or two."

It occurred to me that I hadn't eaten anything since breakfast. I marvelled at how fast the sun set here and the beauty of it as we finished a third Vodka.

Lights from beach bars and restaurants, started to show as the evening darkened, and the background rustle from the tree frogs became evident. The jetty was full so we found a spot on the beach for the dinghy.

"You won't see the rise and fall of tides that you're used to in Ireland," Jack told me. "She'll be here when we get back."

We had a great night eating and drinking, and shared a couple of hours with a group of youngsters off the French cruise ship. I slept like the dead on my first night on Christo.

The next morning we provisioned and took on fresh water, had a late breakfast of bagels, cheese and strong black coffee and set off for Cruz Bay on St John's Island.

Jack called Sam on the radio and he confirmed that he had a replacement fresh water pump. We got a mooring there at four o'clock, and Sam had the pump fitted and was gone by six. Before we went ashore, Jack called his son in Connecticut to get their flight details. I was hosing salt off the cockpit when Jack called from below.

"We're on our own for the trip, Ads. The boys can't make it."

Puzzled, I asked, "What's the problem?"

"A key machine has gone down and production is severely disrupted. Both of them are on it and it's going to take at least a week to sort out and get production back on track."

He looked disappointed because he was looking forward to having them around. Jack had often talked about the many great times they had shared on the boat through all the years from their teens. They had become proficient at all aspects of blue water sailing, navigation and boat handling, through to snorkeling and scuba diving.

"What the hell, they don't need me back at the plant and I don't need them here. I was looking forward to taking it easy and have them do all the work." He wasn't very convincing. "You know, this boat is set up for single handed sailing and I've done it many times, so it's a piece of cake for the two of us." The look on his face as he turned his head told the real story. I knew what was really eating at him.

It had nothing to do with them not coming on the trip. Oh sure, he was disappointed with that but what was really stinging him was the fact that they didn't need him back at the plant to sort out this crisis. The boys had crossed the Rubicon. They were in control and he had to come to terms with this, but it would take some time.

Jack was always the ultimate competitor and hated second best. From earliest times he would lead or try to. Even if we were walking, he would have to step it out. He had seen this coming for some time and here it was.

We went ashore in silence and walked the shoreline till we got to one of his favourite haunts.

"Hi, Jack," we were greeted by an attractive woman with short, straight blond hair and an ample figure.

We were seated at a plastic table on the beach outside a small café. Jack turned and with a huge grin, put an arm around her waist. "Shirley, how are you, my love? Let me introduce you to my old pal, Ads."

"Enough of the old bit," I said as I got up to kiss cheeks.

After a bit of banter and joking (which was another of Jack's fortes), we ordered. That few minutes had shaken the reverie out of Jack and we settled into talking about the immediate jobs to do and planning the trip.

As we left to walk along the beach to the dinghy, Jack stopped, turned to me and said,

"Mixed feelings, Ads. I have been dreading this day in a way, but I am also supremely happy that it's happened and very proud of the boys." He kicked sand and looked out to Christo at her mooring. "However, this couldn't have happened at a better time, because you and I don't get chances like this too often. We'll now have all the time needed for you to do what you have promised for years, to tell me the story of your life. That's the bit I know nothing about. The time before I met you thirty five years ago."

He referred to 1964. We had both gone to live in Ireland only a year before that.

Suddenly he put me in a semi-headlock and stuck his face in mine and said, "Let's go sailing."

Chapter Three

CARIBBEAN

The Genoa snapped full and the main and mizzen stopped flapping as we lounged in the cockpit. We had been on a very gentle broad reach, with only four or five knots of wind, and had not noticed the signs of increased north easterlies.

"Ads, you had better take a break there. We should take advantage of the increased wind to make some progress."

"We're showing 18 knots of wind and there are some squalls ahead," I responded.

Everything about Christo was now taut. It was as if an unseen hand had taken all the slack rigging, sails, sheets et cetera and wound it all up. We busied ourselves in the cockpit, stowing bits and pieces, trimming sails and preparing the boat. I had the helm as Jack went below to check that everything was stowed properly and to close all hatches and windows. He emerged with a couple of orange windcheaters which we donned.

Sailing conditions were now perfect; it was blowing a steady force four or five from the north east. We were heading south on a reach and running with the sea, the colour reflected the blue sky, but dark.

Christo was alive now. She hummed and made sounds like a living thing. Standing in the cockpit at the wheel, you could feel her reacting to the wind and sea and revelling in it. She demanded that you became part of her to make the adjustments to sail and rudder, so that she could reward you. Jack lounged and looking aft caught my eye. No words were necessary.

The little Zodiac caromed along behind on its four metre line. We had made steady progress due south for about three hours with full sails, then towards dusk the wind died to four or five knots and the sails limped and flapped. We had decided to sail through the night and make a course correction in the morning, so we lounged and enjoyed the tropical dusk with Christo on autopilot.

I continued where I left off. "I am a last Anglo Indian."

"What's that"?

"It means that I've British blood mixed with Indian blood."

"Does that mean that you have an English father and an Indian mother or vice versa?"

"No, it doesn't. It means that I am a product of British colonialism in India and that stretches back more than three centuries."

"I don't understand."

"It's a long and complicated story."

"Well I've got all the time in the world."

"It's hard to know where to begin. I haven't given this any real thought, but ok, here it goes. It will probably meander a bit. I'll start with an ending and a beginning."

"Why last?"
"Because I'm the last in a line of Anglo indians."

Chapter Four

SOUTH LONDON - 1947

The morning after Dogsy's electric leap on the siding bridge, I was awakened by a nudge on the shoulder by Dad. Six thirty and pitch black save for the weak light filtering in the doorway from the downstairs' hall light. I crouched tighter in the warm pit that was my bed, stretching those precious extra minutes before I would have to vacate it for the freezing room. My bed was beside the window and I edged the curtain back knowing that I would find the glass stamped with the exquisite swirls and patterns of frost.

Our old red-brick semi was the same as many in the streets of this South London Edwardian suburb. As I crept down to the warm kitchen, my Dad prepared to leave for work. He was a man of ritual and routine. This was a time that I shared with him five mornings a week. In the winter I looked forward to coming into this room because it was always warm and I loved the weak electric light for the glow it imparted. This room was home for our family. It was where everything happened and where our family evolved for the next two decades.

When we first came to the house in the late summer of 1947, there was an ancient black cast iron range in the kitchen, which was part of the house when it was built. I recall that one of the first things that Dad did was to remove it and fit a modern tiled fireplace with a back boiler. This ensured plenty of hot water for our family of seven.

His devotion to ritual was perfect to ensure that this fire never went out. This morning, like every other, he would carefully rake out all the cinders and ashes from the night before, and then methodically stack fresh coal and coke. At that time, and for years after, coal and coke were delivered in hundredweight sacks. I recall our coalman who was quite small, carrying seven or eight of these sacks, one at a time, around the alleyway to our coal bunker at the back of the house. He was black from head to toe from coal dust.

My grandmother would tend it during the day, but at around 6.30pm when he returned from work, he would resume responsibility for the fire. The last act before going to bed was a repeat of the morning, but he would add a layer of ash to the top to slow down the burning. This would ensure that the fire was still alive in the morning. Central heating was unheard of so the kitchen was the only room in the house that was warm and everything happened there.

We didn't speak much in the morning, because, well, he didn't speak much at any time. When he put on his raincoat, flat cap, and trouser clips I knew he was off to work on his Sunbeam bike, which had an enclosed oil bath for the chain. I could hear my mother preparing herself for work upstairs as I went out the front door. It was another very cold and frosty morning, but I loved this time because it was still quiet, dark and a bit mysterious. It felt somehow that it was my special time of the day. Through the smog I could make out the nearest gas street lamps, and the milk cart still about 50 yards away. As I approached I could see the plumes of breath from the cart horse.

"Morning," the milkman greeted me, never using my name.

"Hi, Mr Jones," I replied. There was never any conversation only his instructions.

Within five minutes my fingers were numb from the freezing bottles and by the time the end came an hour later, I was really suffering and ready to run for home to the haven of the kitchen. This routine continued unchanged and I did not need any further instruction. Once a week he would disappear for about 15 minutes into Mrs Carter's house and I would have to wait for him to return. It was only years later that I realised what the distraction was about.

The rear of our house and the others nearby were accessed by an alleyway system that went around the gardens. This was the way that we all went into the house. As I went into the back door everything had changed. My mum had gone to work in the toy factory and the kitchen was alive, as Gran' prepared breakfast for us. My brother and sister got ready for school while little Lily slept.

I dived for Dad's chair next to the fire to warm up and defrost my fingers. Gran sat on the arm of the chair, put her arm around me and took my hands in hers. She held them for several minutes, gently massaging life back into them. That's the way she was.

Chapter Five

SOUTH LONDON

The rail sidings formed the northern limit of our territory with the junior and secondary schools on the western fringe. In between were the recreation park (or 'rec' as we called it) and a dozen or so streets.

The rec was a wonderful place. There were the public and open areas like the playground and tennis courts. The lawns and flower beds, which were lovingly and beautifully maintained, but not much noticed by a nine year old.

Our world was where adult eyes did not penetrate. It was deep in the shrubs and high in the trees. This is where we lived out our fantasies and had our own secret places. This was where we deserted reality and became Tarzan, John Wayne or Roy Rogers, and sometimes you would have to settle to be a hapless Red Indian. These were very special moments and time raced by until you had to cut and run for home.

The streets were Edwardian and named after British heroes like Cavendish, Fortescue, Marlborough, Norfolk, Wilton, and so on. German bombers had flattened many houses in the area, and when our family arrived in 1947, everything was still much as it was by the end of the war.

Only two short years had passed since Londoners had celebrated VE (Victory in Europe) Day and many wartime social organisations were still very active.

One particular bomb site was our favourite playground because it was quite extensive. It covered an area where at least a dozen houses and gardens once stood. Looking back, it was a dangerous place, full of rusted metal and wire, shattered glass and splintered wood; building rubble with cavities and holes that luxuriant vegetation had concealed. There may have also been unexploded ordnance there. Nevertheless, there were loads of places to hide and play out imaginary lives. Our parents put these places out of bounds, but we couldn't resist it.

The shunting line and coal yards were also a very exciting hang out, particularly for older boys. The more daring ones, including Dogsy, would jump from the bridge into the slowly moving wagons. They would have catapults and air guns and would play real cowboys and Indians. The drivers had tried to stop it but had long given up and now ignored it. It's a wonder no one got seriously injured in those times. We would trail them sometimes to watch the action and Jimmy once got nicked by a stray air gun pellet on his scalp just above the ear.

The times of affluence and all that goes with it, were still decades ahead. Our parents, like most of the people in the neighbourhood, were in survival mode. Earnings were carefully allocated to guarantee the essentials. There was very little left for luxuries. Anyway, even if we could afford something, we were all still subject to wartime rationing, so you could not even go into Philips' Corner Shop and buy a simple bar of Cadburys milk chocolate without a ration book.

In winter, it was nearly dark when Kavey and I walked home from school and the lights in the corner shop were like a beacon. Every day we would stop and gape at everything in the window even though we could recite its contents with our eyes closed.

December was the best because it was full of toys such as, colourful boxes of clockwork train sets, dinky cars, sets of toy soldiers, cannons, cowboy outfits and guns, dolls and things for girls. We would look and dream. I recall pressing my nose against the window of the corner shop for weeks on end, gazing at a dinky toy and really wanting it. But it was unreachable. I would have to save for several weeks from my milk round. The aspiration to own that car, the anticipation and waiting, together with the determination to save for it, made it into a project. The great pleasure I experienced when I had enough money to run to Philips' shop and buy that dinky car was immense.

That pleasure of anticipation has gone.

Everything comes too easy now. The times we had to play and relax were taken up doing things. The radio played a large part, and we were avid listeners to the audio soaps of the day. Dad and my brother Keith and I hovered around it for programmes like Dick Barton - Special Agent. Our large all purpose kitchen, dining room, hosted everything from parties and celebrations, to table tennis competitions. But on a daily basis, we would do homework, play games, read, draw, joke, tease and fight each other. We would resurrect old battered toys and rejuvenate them with paint. TV and easy credit has removed most of that.

We had come to live in a country which was alien to what we had been born to and had grown up in. We were also aliens to the residents who were born and grew up here. Immigrants from all parts of the Great British Empire had not started arriving on her shores in any real numbers yet. We attracted attention, and not all of it welcome.

It was the end of August 1947 and we were lucky that it had been a good summer. My sister, Kavey, a year and a half younger, and I were inducted into the local primary school. My brother, Keith went to the secondary school. My parents were overprotective at the start. Coming from a climate that was never cold, they feared we would succumb to cold weather diseases unless we were dressed in about six layers of woollen clothes and hats. We immediately dumped the hats in our neighbour's hedge, to be recovered on the way back home. We sweated through those days until our parents relaxed a bit. The summer of 1947 was very good and quite hot, so it gave us a short time to acclimatise to our new lives. We were not to know it but the winter of 1947/48 was to be one of the coldest of the 20th century in England. In fact, when the first snows arrived we were captivated. Very soon it was about a foot deep and I remember going to the rec along with lots of kids and diving into the deep snow. We had never seen the white stuff before.

However, Dad laid a major responsibility on my shoulders at that time. He insisted that I must escort Kavey safely to and from school, and that I must look out for her there. The trouble was that I was smaller than Kavey. Not only that, but the Indian genes were strongest in me. Actually my brother, Keith, Kavey and little sister, Lily, all had brown hair, green eyes and were quite fair of complexion, (British genes were strongest in them). I was the one who stood out and because I was small and Indian looking, I became a target. At the start it was very confusing and hurtful. The racist name calling was hard to handle, and it was not long before it became physical. When it did, it was a great surprise to me and those who attacked me that I was not such easy prey after all. I was able to defend myself and Kavey. It was not long before this came to the attention of the PE teacher. He decided to introduce me to boxing. This sport was almost as big as football and cricket in the schools at that time. This was great for my psyche, because it commanded a bit of respect amongst the other kids. This undoubtedly helped me through those early years, and enabled me to be relatively strong in dealing with racist barbs. However, that was the positive side.

As time progressed I grew to hate the taunting, abuse and started to try and avoid confrontation. I must have acquired some sort of an inferiority complex. I did things that I could do only by myself and did not involve other people. Whether it was sports or entertainment, I would do things on my own, or with one other person. I seem to have always had one good friend around. Those years, however, dealt me the cards that I have played with for the rest of my life. I do not understand the full spectrum that makes me the person I am, but who does? I believe that my personality and character were determined at that time.

The contrast between Keith and I was big, and always had been. There seemed to be more than two years between us. He was of average size, looked fairly English but more importantly, was an excellent footballer and cricketer. He had great success at school in the sporting and social areas. Not in any way academic, but enjoyed popularity and was always a prefect and captain of this and that.

So it was that Kavey and I gravitated and spent much time together. Lily was not yet three. That first phase time in a new land was traumatic for me and my family. Of course, while we all shared a common experience, we all dealt with it and were affected by it in our own personal ways. The contrasts must have been felt most strongly by my parents and Gran.

By the end of our first school year in July 1948, we had settled into the rhythm of life in our new environment. It was great to be off school for the summer and we set about making the most of it. Strangely, that summer seemed full of sunshine and we were out playing all the time. If it wasn't cowboys and Indians in the rec, we were out at the rail sidings or plotting scrumping in the neighbours' gardens and fruit trees. We had our special friends by now and spent our time with them.

Jimmy and I loved to explore and that was central to most things we did. Our favourite places were the nearby commons of Mitcham and Wimbledon. We would find wooded areas and enact imaginary adventures with imaginary foes. Climbing trees and going as high as possible was a favourite. Sometimes we would bring empty jam jars and home made nets to the ponds and try to catch minnows, sticklebacks and newts.

A couple of weeks after the bridge jump, after I had finished my chores, I walked around to Jimmy's house. It was midday on Saturday and we had the afternoon to have some fun. We decided to walk to Tooting Bec Common. This meant crossing the footbridge. Jimmy's older brother, Bobby had warned him to stay away from it so it was like a red rag to a bull. Still, we exercised caution because Bobby and his pals were older, bigger and stronger than us.

From our angle of approach we could not see anyone who might have been on top of the bridge. Crouching single file along the fences and hedges, we got to the base of the bridge. From here we had a line of sight along one side of the rail track.

"Ding" was the sound of a stone striking the steel of the bridge. Then there was the soft sound of an air gun discharging, followed by the rustling of autumn leaves and branches being disturbed along the track. "Ding", another one struck the bridge followed by an air gun shot. This time there was a shout from the bridge. No, it was more of a scream of pain, actually. It was Dogsy. More rustling among the bushes and some shouting from there to someone on the other side of the tracks ensued.

We heard the sound of a slow moving shunter approaching the bridge and figured it was time to venture up to the first landing so that we could just see Dogsy. The old black shunter chuffed its smoke into the bridge and we used the distraction to run up to the landing. Crouching, we could just see his head. He shut his eyes and coughed till the acrid smoke dissipated. Then quick as a flash, he was up on the parapet looking down at the heaped coal in the first wagon. The second wagon of three was full of coke and when this was under him he jumped down into it.

We scampered up to where Dogsy had been, lay on our stomachs and peered out at the scene. It was like a movie. Dogsy was on his feet, the air rifle loaded and him looking for a target, while the chugger moved at walking pace down the line to the coal yard. The larrup of a catapult firing from the bushes and a stone striking the side of the wagon, caused the gunman to whirl and fire into the bushes. But the hidden attacker had moved on.

Soon there was another thwack from the other side, quickly followed by a scream of pain from Dogsy. This success was celebrated by Bobby who jumped from his cover with arms outstretched, shouted and ran full speed down the track. Another larrup from the other side hit nothing, but the enraged and hurt Dogsy was now firing and reloading as quickly as he could at both sides, until at last a scream from Bobby revealed a hit. So it continued into the distance until we could no longer see anything.

Energised by the action from the tracks, we jogged the quarter mile to the main road, pushing and shoving each other amid laughter. Once over the main road, we were on the common and raced over to the pond. Even though the water had the colour and opacity of bisto gravy, we sauntered around peering into it and hoping to see something alive. The ducks scampered away because of the noise we were making. Tiring of this we ran over to a copse of large trees, looking for the best climber. It turned out to be a mature alder tree which had plenty of stout branches from its trunk. Climbing 20 feet was easy enough but got challenging after that and a look down sent familiar twinges down our legs. Settling for that we made ourselves comfortable in the crook and pulled pears out of our pockets, which we scrumped earlier.

Feeling on top of the world and looking down on everything, we spotted trouble coming. Four kids a few years younger than us, were approaching, looking up at us. At first they stood under the tree shouting questions and doing a bit of jeering, but quickly turned to name calling and abuse. We flung half finished pears at them which only escalated to them flinging badly aimed stones back at us. It didn't take a genius to work out what would happen if one of those struck; it may cause a fall from 20 feet. Their bravado disappeared instantly when we rapidly clambered down, all the while uttering well trained blood curdling Red Indian screams. By the time we got down, they were well out of range but still turning and hurling abuse. We decided it wasn't worth the chase and in any case, by the time we caught them they would have been amongst grown ups and we would have been seen as bullies.

When we first moved into our house the back garden was a wasteland of overgrown beds of rust coloured chrysanthemums amid a mini meadow of weeds and wild flowers. At the end of the garden was a wooden chicken coop with a wire run. Very soon after, Dad bought half a dozen Rhode Island red hens and a cock. We loved messing around with them and collecting eggs from the coop. Every now and then some would hatch and we would have some more chickens. On special occasions Dad would kill one for the table. The first time he did it I insisted on watching the performance and immediately wished I hadn't. It was a particularly gruesome method. The bird's neck would be placed on a piece of wood near the drain and he would simply cut its head off with a sharp knife. He would hold the blood spouting neck over the drain and that was that. The first time we weren't keen to eat that chicken and didn't watch again.

The summer evenings and weekends were great for wandering around and checking out the best places for scrumping. We knew where the best tasting pears, apples, plums and cherries were. Of course it was very risky in most gardens and the chance of getting caught was high. The very best pear tree was at the back of our neighbour's garden which was behind ours. In fact, it was directly behind the chicken run. There was a six foot rusty corrugated iron fence covered in vines and brambles between us. However, we discovered that if we put a plank between our coop and their shed directly behind, we could walk it and pick the pears. We did this several times but they must have noticed something because they laid a trap. They dusted their shed roof with a little white powder and we didn't notice it. The next thing was a knock on the door followed by an accusation. Dad was invited to come and view the evidence but decided it wasn't necessary. A couple of whacks on the tail end, a reduction of sweet rations and an extra chore of polishing brasses was the price. But they were lovely pears. Later we tried a different tack and were particularly nice to them during the cubs' bob-a-job week. They invited us in to go and pick some!

At this stage, Keith was a scout and I was a cub. The first two weeks of August was the planned annual camp and we were going on it. I remember being very excited and looked forward to it for ages. It was an absolutely wonderful experience in the great location of Thursley Common. To me it was a wilderness of forests, streams and fields. We learned lots of outdoors things like tracking, using compasses, searching and identifying wildlife, plants and trees. We had bonfires and sing songs, learned how to cook on campfires and how to make and maintain latrines. It was full of new experiences and lots of fun. A truly great experience for a 10 year old. However, parents and families came to visit us at the middle weekend and homesickness seemed to get the better of us. For a few minutes I bawled into Mum's bosom and wanted to go home, but that passed soon enough.

At the end of that first memorable summer it was school time again and like kids everywhere, we hated the thought of it. However, it was different to last year when it was all new and we were the centre of attention and endured the name calling and fights. This time we went into classrooms filled with kids we knew and had become friends with for the most part.

Mr Harrington, our coach, had entered a team for the upcoming inter schools boxing competitions and I was selected for the lightest weight. We started back in training with much enthusiasm. He was quite old with crew cut grey hair, but was really fit and still had a six pack. He was merciless in his regime and pushed us hard. I recall the smell of the gym and the various mats and equipment. I remember his boxing coaching and especially the medicine ball. He was a revered member of a local boxing club and we would also compete in the inter club competitions.

I learned more than just boxing skills from that man. He taught me about discipline and the value of a strong work ethic. He showed me that success goes hand in hand with determination and perseverance and that talent is not enough by itself. I had a lot of respect for him. During the next school year, when I was 11, I sat the entrance exams for going to a technical school and was successful. I got a place in Wimbledon Technical School for boys. I was to start there when I was 13. At the end of the school term when I was 13, I left my school, the boxing season ended and so did my boxing career.

Those early years in England did something else for me. It taught me to take responsibility for myself and all that I did, and not to depend on or blame anyone else. That was a great lesson, it has stood me well throughout my life and I hope it will for what's left of it. Actually, without knowing it I was starting a new era because my new school was a bus ride away in a different district. So, I was in a school with a slightly elevated status to the standard secondary school and I was making a whole new set of classmates, not all from the locality.

There were two streams of pupils. One wholly dedicated to the construction industry and the other to engineering. We had to make that choice before ever starting at the school. There was no such thing as career guidance or advice in those distant days, so it was more or less like eeny miny mo. That decision was massive because it shaped my life and career. I chose engineering and much later wished I had chosen the other.

This was a turning point and took me out of my comfort zone. I had gotten used to the kids in the local school and now had to go through a new phase of curiosity. The boys were from a wider area but there were a couple that we knew. The difference was that I was a little older and a bit more wary. I found myself withdrawing from possible conflict and it occupied my mind too much. Without realising it, I was rejecting who I was and trying to be like those around me.

All of this started something that became detrimental to my ability to study in classrooms. My attention span had deteriorated and this meant that concentration was hit and miss. Thought processes and focusing on the subject in hand became intermittent. This was obviously disastrous with subjects like maths and science.

Of course, I neither knew nor suspected any of this at the time. The pattern became established and I accepted being in the lower reaches of the class. This persisted for the next three years and I finished with a poor grade diploma and glad to be finished with school.

Chapter Six

COUNTY WEXFORD, IRELAND - LATE 1930S

The same year I was born in Asansol, West Bengal, a baby girl was born in a cottage in County Wexford, Ireland. She was born healthy and with no complications, to Sean and Elizabeth Doyle. It was their fourth daughter.

It was early December, but the weather had not yet turned wintry. It was late afternoon and the midwife had finished cleaning up. It was dusk, and she was anxious to set out on her bicycle back to the town. She had celebrated with Sean by enjoying a cup of tea with a shot of whiskey in it.

Rita, the eldest daughter, had been minding Maria and Kitty in the back field during the birth, and they were allowed back in as the midwife was leaving. With beaming and flushed faces, they gathered around their mother's bed and gazed at their new sister in wonder. They took it in turns to hold the tiny hands and stroke her head.

"We have decided to call her after me," said Elizabeth. It didn't take long for this to become Lizzie. By the time that they got bored with the new arrival, it was dark. Sean had lit two lamps to add to the light of the fire in the hearth. It was not long before family, neighbours and friends started arriving with gifts, food, bottles of stout and lemonade for the children. There was great celebration and laughter that evening.

The cottage was typical of those built in the early part of the century. There was a small porch which had a room on each side. To the right was Sean and Elizabeth's bedroom. To the left was the all purpose room with an open fire. In one corner was a narrow staircase which led to a small loft room, with a little window in the gable wall. There was no water, drainage or electricity in the house. Water was drawn from a well down the lane and there was a tiny outhouse dry toilet in the yard. It would be another 25 years and more before electricity became available in the area.

The cottage was located up a lane off the main road which linked Wexford Town with the coast and the villages and townlands. It was also on the upslope of a hill, and the lane continued past the house to access the higher slopes for sheep. There were half a dozen houses within a half mile radius of the cottage, one of which was the farm where Sean worked. There existed a closeness that was common in this sort of community. It was at times like this that it paid off. The women had taken over some of Elizabeth's chores for the past week and would continue that until she was strong again.

At that time the Irish economy was totally dependent on agriculture. Farming was also very labour intensive and farmer's dependent on local labour. Sean's duties were general and changed with the time of day and year. One thing did not change and that was work from dawn to dusk, except in the mid-summer months. Because of that he left the cottage before dawn and returned after dark. It was a very physical and grinding one which demanded being out in all weathers every day.

The work was casual in nature and at times when there was not much to do, there was no work.

After dinner and an hour relaxing by the fire, he would walk down to the small pub at the crossroads. This was a room about 20 feet square. There was a simple wooden counter just inside the door. Behind that there were some wall shelves with popular brands of Irish whiskey, glasses, bits and pieces and an old radio occupied the corner. This was operated by a car battery which sat on the shelf under the radio.

The floorboards were covered with sawdust and beer crates served as seats. The clientele was purely local and entirely male. It was also only regulars, so everyone knew everyone and all there was to know about each other.

Joe Sinnott and his wife, Jess owned the pub and lived over it. They were in their late 50s, but had no family. They ran the pub together, spending every evening behind the bar. A stranger walking into the room would quickly but subtly become the center of attention. They would be welcomed and could not help but be impressed with the wit and banter amongst the locals. They would not immediately be aware that a lot of it was barbed or cynical or plain gossip.

The pub and the church were the hub of the community and had been for centuries past. The county town was the farthest most people would travel and the outside world made no impact. Sean's brothers, Jim and Paddy would join him. At weekends the room would be packed, hazy with cigarette smoke. The brothers had grown up on pint bottles of stout and when they could afford it, occasionally chased with a small whiskey. Jokes and laughter would bounce around the room in bursts, in between times of quiet conversation.

Best of all would be when Bertie Hassett would arrive with his melodeon. He would take up station on a beer crate in the corner opposite the bar and would be joined by Jess on another crate with her fiddle. Paddy would take the bodhrán off its nail on the wall behind the bar. On these occasions the craic would be mighty and would run on past closing time. Though all would partake in the singing, there were favourites and Sean's rendition of "The Galway Shawl" was high on the list. Most times Mickey Spillane would clear a space and provide 15 minutes of tap dancing.

The brothers lived within a mile of each other, but once they walked out of the pub they each took a different road from the crossroads. Even though there was very little night time traffic in those days, the roads were narrow, twisty and had no hard shoulders. They were extremely dangerous to walk on in the dark.

In years to come the families were to lose two young men in this way. Sean was a year younger than Paddy and the two of them spent all their spare time together up to the time they met the girls who were to become their wives.

Chapter Seven

COUNTY WEXFORD - 1920S

Sean and Paddy were in their early 20s and the time of year was mid-summer. It was a time when daylight stretched to within an hour of midnight. The crops in the fields were well sown and in mid growth. The first cut of hay had been done. After the cows had been milked, there was still several hours of daylight left. They would sometimes either walk or cycle to the next village or Wexford Town. There they would hang out where other young people did in the hope of meeting someone. Most of the time nothing much happened, but from time to time they would meet girls the same way that young men did the world over.

It was on one such occasion that they cycled to a nearby village called Taghmon. A group of travelling singers from Dublin was due to perform in the village. The weather was perfect, and the closer they got to the village, the more people they passed on their bikes. It became obvious that the performance was going to draw a large crowd. They decided to leave their bicycles in a ditch outside the village and walk in. As they strolled the few hundred yards in the sunshine, they were high in spirit and anticipation. They had a haversack with sandwiches for the day and enough money to buy a couple of bottles of stout. The day was perfect in every way: warm sunshine, a few small white clouds to break the entire blue sky and a light breeze to keep everyone cool.

The musicians were to perform in a field adjacent to a large hay barn so that if the weather turned nasty, they would continue in the barn. Many people had gathered and sat or stood in groups waiting. The boys knew a lot of people there, some well, others as acquaintances. There was a lot of banter and calling going on. Of course their eyes were out on stalks looking for the best place to settle down.

There were families, young and old, as well as young single people. It was Sean whose eyes made contact with the eyes of a girl around his own age. She stood with a family group under a large ash tree. She looked away in shyness, but his gaze was fixed and he took in the way she wore her red brown hair. It was shoulder length in loose curls, with the sides clipped up over her ears. She was of medium height and very slim but shapely. Her print dress had puff sleeves and was tight at the waist with a little red belt. Sean was gobsmacked!

Paddy was engaged in loud conversation with someone a distance away and had not noticed Sean's preoccupation. When he did, he followed Sean's gaze and grinned. He nudged him into action and they sauntered casually around to where the family had settled down. They were handsome brothers, both around the same height, but Sean was slightly taller. They had straight fair hair, which had been liberally applied with brilliantine, combed flat with a centre parting for Sean but a side one for Paddy. As they sat down they took off the jackets of their dark well worn suits, to reveal their white cotton shirts and braces.

The musicians arrived and started their performance. A wooden stage had been set up, which was just large enough for them plus space for a local tap dancing group to perform. This was to go on all afternoon, with the main group taking breaks which would be filled by local performers. The local publican had assumed the role of compere and took every opportunity to inject local stories with some dubious wit. He would, of course, suffer much cat-calling.

It was one of those days that the brothers would always have vivid memories of, especially Sean. His eyes rarely strayed from the girl who had entranced him. She had rewarded him with many fleeting glances from her grey eyes. His mind absorbed nothing of what was taking place around him. He wondered how he could make contact with her. He had ruled out a direct approach because she was with her family, but probably more so because he was afraid of rejection. All the possible options churned away in his head and as the afternoon wore on, fear that they may leave early, gripped him.

Paddy had deserted him to join some friends, but now he heard his name being called. Paddy and his companions were walking towards the village and he was beckoning Sean to join them. Reluctantly he arose and as he did, she turned and looked at him. He wanted to kneel beside her and introduce himself. Instead, he involuntarily turned and started walking away, cursing himself as he went.

Moments after, he knew with great certainty that this was to be his partner for life. He set about finding out who the family was and where they were from. The rest of the day and evening was spent fooling around and having a lot of fun, before they decided to pick up the bikes and head for home.

Chapter Eight

TIMELINE - COUNTY WEXFORD

It was 1926 and only four years had passed since Ireland's declaration of independence. Memories were vivid and very fresh of all aspects of the British occupation. People were still getting used to the feeling of freedom. It really did not make any difference to their way of life or affect their daily routines in any significant way. It did, however, create a massive euphoria in the knowledge that the British had finally gone.

The Doyle family lived in a mid 19th century thatched cottage, typical of many in the country. It had a half door at the front with two small windows, one on each side of the door. It was whitewashed on the outside. The floor inside was flagstones and the cottage consisted of the main living room and a bedroom. Above the bedroom was a loft area, which was divided into two small rooms. Paddy and Sean shared one of these small rooms and their older sister, Kay had the other. Jim had flown the coop a year before to live in Wexford Town. Their father, John, had been active in the resistance from 1912, but was now in the final stages of terminal cancer andbedridden.

Kay and her mother, Violet tended to all the household chores and the half acre field behind the cottage. To one side was a small shelter of mud and lath with an enclosure, which housed a pig. They also had some hens and a cock which roamed free. The field was tilled, where they grew their own potatoes, cabbages, carrots and onions. Sean and Paddy both worked on nearby farms and would bring home milk and butter.

It did not take long for Sean to discover who the girl who had come to dominate his mind. She lived near Taghmon with her family and her name was Elizabeth McMahon. He was very fortunate that he had sparked the same feelings in her as he felt for her. When they finally met for the first time they both knew their destinies were made.

A year later Sean married Elizabeth. It was a simple wedding in the Catholic Church in Taghmon. Sean was fortunate that his employer had a vacant cottage and was happy to rent this to the couple.

A year after Sean married Elizabeth, Paddy married her sister, Mary who was a year older than Elizabeth. They were to have seven children, three boys and four girls, in fairly quick succession. It was a sad fact but not uncommon in those days, that both women were to suffer four miscarriages each.

They lived in a similar cottage, down Sinnott's bohereen, not more than half a mile away. Both men were labourers on neighbouring farms and the women raised their children, tended the households and vegetable gardens. Their lives were centred in the local couple of miles, and this was absolutely normal for the time. The children over four all attended the local national school, a mile and a half down the road.

Elizabeth and Mary were separated by only a year and they were very close, almost like twins. They would see each other most days, unless the weather was particularly bad. They loved each other's company and shared many things. They did not see themselves as isolated in any way; rather they felt a deep sense of belonging to a close knit community. All the working class people in the parish felt this. At this time, people did not travel outside their parish, except on rare occasions. Transportation was primitive and costly. The outside world did not figure much in people's minds, and the only real contact with it was through the medium of radio. Since there was no electricity, the batteries were saved and the radio was only used for a limited time each evening. It was also only the people who could afford a car battery and have the means to recharge it that had a radio. The time was still like it had always been; all the means of communication, like radio, television, telephone, and indeed electricity, were still many years away for most country people.

The hearth and turf fires were the focal point, as was the pub for the men. People did what they had done for millennia, they had conversation. Their minds were fed by their lives and community. They lived by the light of day and the weather. They had oil lamps and the firelight. They gossiped and joked about themselves, their neighbours and friends in the good times. They also had very difficult and hard times, and they battled through these as best they could. This was where the community paid off and help was at hand.

So it was that legends were born, great stories told and perpetuated about local heroes and events. It was also true that deep rooted enemies were made and persisted. There were dark secrets in many households about unmentionable things. People feared disgrace and gossip more than anything else. Most things that should not have happened in working class families were concealed at all costs to save embarrassment and disgrace.

One early evening Sean arrived home from work; it was dusk and late November. It was one of those still evenings with a fog on the hill behind them, and promised a hard frost that night. He walked in the door and hung his cap on a hook inside the door. Elizabeth was at the bellows beside the fire. They greeted each other with a glance and no more. He took his seat in an old wooden armchair beside the fire. There was a stack of wood and sticks to one side and a small reed basket of turf beside that. Replenishment of this was one of Elizabeth's many daily duties. A cast iron grid hinged from the side over the fire. On it was a black pot with a lid. She had some vegetables and potatoes cooking along with a crubeen for flavour. A fresh log sent out sparks from the embers.

"Kay is not too well," Elizabeth spoke as she lifted the lid to stir the stew. "She was down with Mary in the morning and complained about getting sick a lot." She sat beside him on a small stool and looked at his face in the flickering firelight. He was staring at it as he said,

"What do you think is wrong with her?"

"I hope that it isn't what I think it might be."

He turned to her with a questioning look. "You know she went to a dance with Molly Breen last month in Wexford Town. They met up with the fella who runs the bookies shop on the corner of the new line. Well, she has seen him a few times since. He has a car and he has brought her a few places, but she hasn't seen him for a couple of weeks."

He looked at her with a look of dismay but said nothing. As he turned to stare at the embers again he said, "I'll walk over to the house after work tomorrow and talk to her. Let's hope that it's a false alarm. If it's true then there's trouble ahead."

The yellow light cast by the two paraffin lamps added to the glow of the fire. The one that illuminated the table where the children sat playing and working, also uplighted the Sacred Heart on the wall. Sean stared at it as his mind worked at the prospect of his sister's situation. The chatter and noise of three girls aged from three to seven at the table washed over him. The youngest, a year old lay asleep in the worn out pram. He had rolled a cigarette, and had lit it from a stick from the fire. He mused on the problem and allowed his mind to develop the probability of disgrace for them all.

The two eldest girls had gone to a neighbour's house where one of their friends lived. When they returned, Elizabeth served the stew with some soda bread. This was a daily routine they shared and apart from school and work, this was their whole world. Each one of them had a private world inside their heads, but together they were an interdependent unit. Beyond that, the extended families formed another interdependent unit. Sean's sister's problem would have an adverse effect on them all.

Later, when they were all in bed, Sean and Elizabeth lay in each other's arms and whispered their thoughts to one another. The two youngest shared their room and the four eldest the other room. Not long after, a gentle burr from her breathing told him she was asleep but it was quite a while before oblivion took him.

The next day Sean cycled the mile to his mother's house where Kay lived. He need not have bothered at all because she gave no hint that there was any kind of a problem. If there was one, then it was clutched tightly to her chest. Revelations and openness were not the order of the day; secrets were. However, this was not one that could be denied indefinitely and Sean knew the truth.

Life carried on as normal for them all for another five or six months when Kay disappeared. She had apparently gone to England to her maternal aunt in London, who was recovering from an operation and needed care.

The truth was much nearer home. In fact, she was in a convent in Wexford Town where she would give birth in secret, and the baby would be taken for adoption by way of an orphanage. Such was the power and influence of the Church and its collusion with the State. She would never experience the joy of motherhood as a single person.

The next five years would pass and would see the devastation of the lives of Sean, Paddy and their families.

Chapter Nine

DISASTER
COUNTY WEXFORD - EARLY 1940S

Three years later, Elizabeth lay in her bed in a foetal position. Her pallid skin stretched across her cheekbones like parchment. Her once sparkling eyes half closed in pain and the anticipation of the next bout of coughing that would rack her emaciated body.

Kay sat on a stool and watched her. She had been there for over an hour and in between the coughing and bringing up phlegm and blood, she had talked to her. Kay knew that Elizabeth had not long to live and the two women had developed a closeness that was to be a great comfort to Elizabeth during her last months. Kay had confided to her about her baby and told her the whole story about her sorrow and loss.

Tuberculosis was rampant in Ireland, particularly in poor rural areas. The damp, cold winters aided and abetted the disease. Like thousands of others she had contracted it but denied it for as long as she could. She fought it and worked herself harder than ever for as long as she could. The time came too quickly when she could stand no more, and she took to her bed. Her two eldest daughters and Kay took turns to help her and took on the household chores. Sean had to continue his work, but would sit with her in the evenings by lamplight. He and the children had to share the horror of her terrible coughing. They all knew that the little body could not survive this for much longer and in a way, they wished it would come and bring final peace to her.

Strangely, she recovered a little bit for two days and the little ones cheered up greatly, not knowing that it was just a fleeting moment.

The moment passed and she became worse than ever for only a day. The time came at two in the afternoon when Kay was with her. She lay asleep, her face creased in pain, when there came a little shudder. Kay watched as the creases left her face and Elizabeth's body seemed to relax. Kay knew that she had gone from this life. The old word for the disease was consumption, and it had truly consumed this once beautiful young woman, not yet 40.

When she stopped crying she got up from the stool and went over to the bed. She turned Elizabeth on to her back and straightened out her body. Then she tidied the bedclothes around her and went down the stairs to where three-year-old Annie was playing, unaware of the moment.

Kay put their coats on, took her hand and they walked down the lane to the Sinnott's house. She knew that the other girls would not be home from school for another two hours at least. One of the farm labourers working near the house went to the lower field where Sean was repairing a fence.

Sean walked home with Kay and carried Annie in his arms. He loved the fragrance of fresh air from her hair, but it could not stop his tears. She chatted in total innocence to her dad but her words fell on deaf ears as Sean trudged up the gravel path. When Rita came home from school with her three sisters, they were not in their usual high spirits because they knew that their mother was very ill and the older girls were expecting the worst.

Rita went into the house first and told the others to wait outside until she called, but Lou' had been crying for her mother and was having none of it. She dashed past Rita but not past her dad's arms. He sat at the stool and put his arms around her but looked up into Rita's questioning face, whose eyes filled with tears as she understood the look on her father's face. She was rooted to the spot as Lou struggled and screamed for her mother and Sean let her go as Rita ran to her mother's room. The other girls came into the house as they heard their sister scream.

Sean sat and held his head in anguish at the sound of the crying coming from around his wife's bed. Kay, who had been standing at the door, went into the bedroom and took charge of the girls and did her best to comfort them. Mrs Sinnott had sent word to others in the family, especially to Jim, Paddy and Mary. Soon they would all arrive at the cottage and the reality would slowly settle over them.

Lizzie was always one to spend time on her own and loved to walk in the fields, day dreaming. Now she took herself quietly to the lane and walked slowly up the hill towards the end of the lane. It was dusk, but she was very familiar with her surroundings and not at all afraid.

She was still crying, but the impact of her mother's death had not registered in her young mind. She plucked at dead seed heads as she went and tried hard to think of things other than her mother lying cold in her bed. She really could not think of her as never coming back. That was a leap too far.

A hare ran across the lane from the field to the left and into the heather and ferns leading up the hill. As she watched it disappear into cover she heard the crunching footsteps behind her, and turned to see her father reach down and pick her up. His face was something that she had never seen before.

Her dad was a rock. He was the universe to her and was capable of anything. His shovel-like hands toughened from continual labour and his powerful frame was like a safe harbour to her. Now he looked at her close face and could not contain his tears. She told him not to cry and wiped the tears from his reddened eyes. As she did it, her little frame racked with sobbing, and they held each other for a long time before he turned and carried her back.

Lou was a highly strung child and had worn herself out with crying and screaming for her mother to come back. When Annie was put to bed, Lou went too and they quickly went to sleep. Lizzie and Kitty went soon after, but Rita and Maria stayed up with the adults to share in the mourning that had started and would continue until the burial and wake in three days time.

Father Maguire had arrived earlier, had heard her last confession and given the last rites. Sean's mind was a kaleidoscope, ranging in thoughts from the immediate grief and loss of his beloved wife to a thousand other things, but all associated with the event. Not least of these was the care of the children. For the moment all was in hand, Kay and Mary had everything under control. How wonderful to have them, and for the time being he was content with that. Sean did not possess a mind that looked too far into the future, but that was probably because of his background and culture that was quite unchanging and stable. He was not a dreamer in the way that Lizzie was or her mother before her.

In the days to come, Sean had the crutch of family and friends to rely on as well as the parish priest, Father Maguire. Sean was encouraged to attend mass each morning before the funeral and the priest was to become a familiar figure to the children and visited daily.

Chapter Ten

SUNDERED FAMILY COUNTY WEXFORD

In the days and weeks that followed, Sean and each of his daughters adjusted to the death of Elizabeth in different ways and the home never really felt the same again. Rita and Maria assumed charge of the house and their sisters and made sure that all the routines were continued. Kitty and Lizzie helped as best they could. Lou and Annie took longer to come to terms with it, but could not really understand the loss of their mother.

Sean withdrew from reality and worked from dawn to dusk, leaving everything to his daughters. He spent more time in the pub, only going home to sleep and at home he would sit staring at the fire. The children coped as best they could without bothering him. There was a total hopelessness about the man and he was shutting everything out. He could not face reality or look ahead and plan a future. The lives of this family were being played out with no one in control.

The weeks turned into months and it was late autumn now. The days were shortening and it was getting colder and wetter. The added burdens were starting to take their toll on the older girls and there was friction among them.

The daily chores of getting water from the well and foraging for wood for the fire, cleaning and cooking were heaped on walking miles to and from the national school. The sisters were rarely good humoured and often at odds with each other, but were at least vocal and expressed their emotions.

Lizzie was different. She had withdrawn into herself since her mother's death. Without Sean to provide some strength and guidance, she went into a sort of dream world of denial and pretence, a little bit like her father. She was unforgiving of her mother for leaving them. The void that Elizabeth left behind was like a black hole. It was all Lizzie could see and she could see no glimmer of light to fill it. She groped her way through every day, looking forward to the blessed relief of her bed at night to cry herself to sleep.

The bedroom was tiny and damp. It had two makeshift bunk beds. Maria and Kitty had a bed each and the youngest slept top to toe in the other two bunk beds. The nights were the time that all of them retreated into their own world of worry and fear at the uncertainty of the time. It was a loft room and had a tiny window on the gable end with no curtain. Lizzie could see a small patch of sky and if it was a clear night, a few stars would twinkle at her and she would focus on them to help her dream and forget reality. On cold mornings the glass would be patterned with swirls of frost, and her demons would return.

Sean left the house in the dark before dawn and he left the big black kettle on the stove. Rita and Maria took it in turns to get up first and Lizzie could hear whoever it was clattering around, preparing porridge for all of them. Every now and then she would call them all to get washed and dressed. Each would get a bowl of the oats and sometimes, bread and butter. When they were ready, Maria would hurry them out of the house and they would set off on the mile and a quarter trudge to school, whatever the weather. Maria understood the need for routine and she clung to it for all their sakes.

On a frosty, dry morning in November, the six girls strung out in single file, making their way to the little national school, with Lou and Annie bringing up the rear. They tried to keep on the gravel or tarmac to keep their feet dry. If their feet got wet on the way to school they would be cold and wet for the day. At least there were no puddles around because it hadn't rained for days. They got to school in time and had a perfectly ordinary day. Little did they know that it was to be anything but a normal day; it was to be one that all their lives changed forever.

The day passed uneventfully at school and they chatted with their friends outside before the journey home. They were at the fork in the road, only a quarter of a mile from the cottage, when they caught sight of Kay coming towards them.

"Hi Kay," they called and greeted each other.

"Where are you going?" quizzed Kitty.

"I've come to meet you all and I'm coming home with you."

Annie ran up to her and was grabbed up into her arms. She gave Annie an unusually long hug and kiss, which didn't go unnoticed by Kitty or Lizzie. They looked at each other in puzzlement, but carried on up the lane dragging their heels. When they got within sight of the cottage, they also got sight of a large black car parked outside. Visits by the priest had tailed off over the past month, but he had been to the house two days ago. However, none of the girls were privy to the discussions he had been having with Sean. He had arrived in the evening with Kay and the three of them had walked up the lane in order to have their conversation away from young ears. The children were about to find out what those visits were all about.

Rita and Maria were old enough to be very worried about the visit and were too choked up with emotion to speak. Kitty gripped Kay's arm and asked,

"What's the priest doing here again today?"

"Hush, Kitty, you will know soon enough. Your dad will tell you all together when we get in."

Rita went back to Lizzie and Lou, took them by the hands and brought them in. Maria held Kitty's hand as they all entered the cottage. There was wood burning in the hearth and it gave a welcoming cheery glow to the darkening room. Sitting in the chairs on each side of the fire were Sean and the parish priest.

Father Maguire had a benign priestly smile on his face, but it wasn't echoed by Sean. He did not look at any of the children, but stared at the floor. Kay looked at him in fear and this fear transmitted itself to Annie and Lou who looked at her, tears welling.

"Dad, what's the matter, what's wrong?" Rita posed the question that they all wanted to ask.

Sean continued staring at the ground and gave no response. Father Maguire looked at Sean for a few seconds, before putting his mug of tea on the floor and getting to his feet. He looked taller than he was in his black suit. The top of his head was like a billiard ball, red and shiny with sweat from sitting at the fire. The children turned to face him and focused on his sharp grey eyes. He was about to speak, but Lizzie broke ranks and rushed over to Sean.

"Daddy, what's wrong with you?" she squeaked, clasping his face in both her small hands and lifted his head to face her. Eyes, reddened from anguish, he looked back and swept around his gathered children, but only for a moment. Lizzie's question remained unanswered, but they knew there would be no answer.

"Children, I will speak for your father," began the priest in his best intonation. "Don't be alarmed, there is nothing to fear. In fact we're going for a nice drive, which I'm sure you will enjoy." He smiled and paused for a response. All he got was six puzzled faces staring at him. He reached out and took Kitty's hand before continuing. "You are going to meet some very nice nuns in the town and you can think of it as a holiday." As he said this he led Kitty out of the house and gestured the others to follow. Kay also shushed the others outside and they were all herded towards the big black car. She went back for Lizzie who would not leave Sean.

Lizzie had her right arm around his neck. and looked defiantly at Kay, tightening her grip.

"Get away from me!" she screamed.

Lou wrenched free and ran back to her dad. Tears of anguish flowed from the eyes of the two infants and the broken man. The priest opened the rear door of the car and ushered Rita, Maria and Kitty in. Rita also had Annie with her and the door was closed to shut out the sounds from the house. It took many minutes for Kay and the priest to console and persuade the two children to join the others in the car. Before they had time to think, the car had been started and it was rolling and bumping slowly down the lane towards the main road. Rita had time to turn and look back to the cottage, but there was no sign of Sean.

This would be the last time the children would ever see their home.

It was a time that rural Ireland was gripped in obedience and great deference to the Catholic Church. This enabled the law to remove babies, children and adolescents from their parents and homes. They were then committed to life in an institution run by the clergy.

The Church and State had colluded and arrived at the decision that the Doyle children should be removed from their father's care and put into the care of an institution. There it was. There was a numbness that quenched the myriad of questions in the children's minds. They travelled the few miles in silence and arrived at the courthouse in the town.

The intimidation imposed by the grim interior was enhanced by the presence on high of the judge. The frightened children huddled together on a bench and were completely unaware of their fate. The judge, representing the State, pronounced that the six girls would from that moment, be removed from the care of their father. The legal custody of Rita (12), Maria (10), Kitty (eight), Lizzie (six), Lou (five), and Annie (four) would from now be passed to the Sisters of Mercy in the Industrial School, Wexford.

After the brief procedure, a nun took charge and they walked the short distance to large black cast iron gates which were the entrance to the high grey granite walled "school". An old man let them in and the gates clanged shut behind them.

The mother superior of the institution had prepared a blue linen bag with a name tag for each child. These had been given to the priest and he in turn had asked Kay to fill them with essential clothes in advance of this day. Now these were taken out of the car boot and given to each child when they arrived.

They stood together with Kay looking up at the huge stone building in front of them as Father Maguire went up the granite steps to ring the polished brass bell beside the entrance door. It took a couple of minutes before the door opened and a young nun appeared. The priest had a few words with her and turned to Kay asking her to wait a minute, before disappearing into the building with the nun. She brought him to the matron's office who instructed the young nun what to do.

Kay was doing her best to pacify the sisters when the nun reappeared with two others. In a cheerful but brisk manner, one took the hands of Rita and Maria, another the hands of Kitty and Lizzie, and the last took the hands of Lou and Annie. They went up the steps and disappeared into the dark hallway, leaving Kay standing, sobbing and guilt-ridden, to return home.

Once inside, each nun with her two charges brought them down hard echoing hallways in different directions and up staircases to different floors.

At that point the Doyle family was now sundered. Each pair was installed on different floors in different age groups and would not see each other, except on rare occasions.

So began their incarceration. They were to spend their young lives in this industrial school until the age of 15 and know no other life.

At this time they were all in a state of shock and knew not where to turn, especially the younger ones. Who would give them comfort or reassurance? Who would hug them or answer questions? All they had that first night in their large dormitory was a pillow to cry into. That's the way it was from now on.

Lizzie and her sisters' lives had been cast into this place where there was no freedom or choice. It was decreed that there was only one life choice for them when they left at 15. That was to enter into the service of other more privileged people as maids or servants.

There was no point in providing a full educational facility. They would concentrate on household skills at the expense of academic subjects. After all, they would not be sitting for the normal state examinations. They had been a family but were now denied their rights of a normal family upbringing and the care of their siblings and father.

On top of that, they were also denied the educational rights of all Irish citizens and the opportunity to choose their way forward in life.

The six children had been born into a close family environment. First, they had lost the love and comfort of their mother at a very young age when they most needed her. While still in shock and bewilderment, they lost the man who would protect and love them. At the same time they were dragged away from their hearth and home, and placed in a stone cold heartless place.

Finally, the one thing left to them was also taken away. They would no longer have each other for comfort. Separated into different age groups, each was now on her own and had to endure that finality. All that was left for comfort was their pillow at night.

They were denied one other thing, which was the most precious. They were to survive their childhood and adolescence without it:

Love.

Chapter Eleven

INCARCERATION COUNTY WEXFORD

Long days and longer nights stretched out in front of Lizzie and her sisters. These built into weeks and months while they were inexorably institutionalised by the nuns. The sobbing and anguish of the nights, longing to be back at home together gradually disappeared as the weeks turned into months. The discipline, work, hardness and lack of contact between the sisters wore them down.

Fear was quickly embedded into them. It was the sight of physical punishment and cruelty inflicted on anyone committing even the slightest indiscretion. Lizzie very soon understood the rules and complied in order to minimise physical abuse.

It was a regime of stark hard work day in, day out. They were working for the nuns, washing and cleaning everything. Darning and sewing, repairing and doing it all over again. Scrubbing floors, preparing potatoes and root vegetables and working in the laundry.

The bizarre effect of this brutal regime was that the rare times when they were allowed recreation time or have an outing, the girls felt privileged.

Weeks turned into years. Rita spent two years there before being released into the world. The nuns arranged a position for her as a servant to a wealthy family in Dublin. Two years later, a similar arrangement was made for Maria in County Wicklow.

They had been well trained to fulfil the servile role of cleaning, washing, fetching, cooking, child minding and other menial tasks. But now they were very happy girls. No longer were they incarcerated behind those grey walls. No longer did they live in fear of punishment. The small amount of time off from their duties they used to savour the world around them. It was unbelievable to be free to go where they wanted, spend what little money they earned, befriend whoever they liked, become like the people all around them and most of all, to have the freedom of choice.

For Kitty, Lizzie, Lou and Annie, life carried on without change. However, Annie, who was always sick, had progressively gotten worse. Her weak chest never improved; instead she suffered pneumonia and pleurisy. In time she was confined to a room on the top floor and her sisters were not allowed to visit her. When they were out in the yard playing or exercising, they would look up and see her emaciated face looking down at them from the window. They would send her messages and try to make her smile.

This went on for more than a year and then suddenly she didn't appear again. One day they were brought up to her room but could only look at her through the glass in the door and were not allowed in. Annie looked at them with sunken eyes and a grey face that only had a trace of a smile. They didn't need to be told that she would not live much longer. The three sisters clung to each other and sobbed their hearts out. Memories of their dear mother in her death bed came flooding back. Annie passed away two days later.

Two or three times a year Sean would be allowed to visit them and on rare occasions, he could bring two of them back home with him for a weekend. He would go up in the ass and cart. This day he had come up to collect Lizzie and Lou.

Lou was a very lively girl and was jigging around and giggling at everything in anticipation.

Lizzie was very beautiful if a bit thin. She had striking red hair, and a captivating smile that revealed deep dimples in her freckled cheeks. Her long hair was most often worn in two plaits, which were sometimes looped on top of her head.

That's the way she wore it on this Saturday morning in early September. It was a glorious late summer's day, and looked set to last, but this was Ireland and you never could be sure. She sat beside her younger sister, their legs dangling over the seat of the cart. They chatted and laughed at the joy of the day and at the thought of the four mile journey to the cottage.

The ditches were a riot of foliage and colour. The dense shrubbery of hawthorn, ash, elder and blackberry hid a view of the landscape beyond. Between the hedges and the tarmac the wild flowers and grasses ran on seamlessly and forever, and passed by under their legs. Patches of snowy white wild garlic brushed against delicate dandelion puffballs. Sweeping grasses and wild oats were interspersed with yellow buttercups and tall white daisies. The blue roof over their heads was daubed with scudding white cumulus.

Sean Doyle sat up front with the reins in his hands. They led to the bridle in the mouth of the small ageing grey ass. He frequently turned and smiled at his two daughters. The two girls talked amongst themselves and were in wonderment about being free in the lovely world. Both girls wore faded print frocks, and had brown leather sandals on their feet without socks. The journey would take about an hour and they amused themselves by chatting, joking and plenty of laughter. Lizzie was well into her tenth year and Lou was nearly nine.

This perfectly ordinary country scene was playing out and the people they passed and greeted, weren't aware of the joy of hope and happiness bursting in the hearts of the two girls.

Chapter Twelve

LIZZIE'S LOST CHILDHOOD

War had raged in Europe and the Far East. Untold misery had been cast on the earth. Unspeakable things had been committed to millions of innocent people. When itended in 1945, much of the world lay in ruins and poverty was everywhere.

All of this went unnoticed by Lizzie and her sisters in Wexford, except for one German bomb which fell in Campile.

The drudgery of their lives continued throughout. Rita had left by then when she reached 15. The nuns had found her a position in Dublin working as a servant for the family of a senior civil servant. There were three young children to be looked after as well as general household chores.

Rita was very happy to be released from the confines of the institution. However, she was a feisty person and was determined to look for a job that would give her much more freedom. She quickly found that these were hard times and job prospects were very few for a person with her background. She had to stick it out for more than a year before an opportunity came along. She had befriended Mrs Doyle, the owner of her local shop, and who was an elderly widow and enjoyed chatting with Rita.

Her husband had died six months before and she was having difficulty coping. One day when Rita was there buying some groceries, Mrs Doyle, looking tired, asked her if she knew anyone reliable who was looking for a job. Strangely the possibility had never entered Rita's head, but it only took her a second to absorb the question and blurt out her response. Rita had to wait for a replacement before she could go and work for Mrs Doyle.

Two years after Rita left Wexford, Maria's turn came. She was sent to a house in Co. Wicklow and was to stay there for several years. It was to a young family that was steeped in country life. There was much natural affection and to her joy they included Maria in this.

She quickly shed the misery of the past four years. The wonderful family she worked for and lived with coupled with a real sense of freedom, lifted her heart. The house was on 10 acres of woodland and pasture. It was also within walking distance of a small village and a bus service to county towns and Dublin. She wasn't shackled to a regime of work but rather became a working member of the family. The children had ponies and dogs and Maria loved to have fun with them.

At least once a month she would go and spend a day off with Rita who had a bedsit near the shop. They would ramble to the harbour and along the seafront talking about their new lives and would never talk about the past. In the evening Rita would introduce her to some friends and they would all go dancing. Of course, most of the talk would be about the opposite sex and there would be comparisons and possibilities. Maria hadn't met anyone yet or had any experience with boys so she listened avidly.

On her third visit to Rita she was stunned to hear that she had met a boy and had been on a couple of dates with him. She really liked him. Maria was full of questions and Rita was amused by the innocence of some of them. Maria squealed with delight when Rita told her that she would meet him that afternoon. They would have to get a bus to the village and he would meet them there.

His name was Frank and Killiney Hill was his favourite place. He planned to share the wonderful views from the top of the hill with Rita. It was a headland which jutted over the bay and there was a panorama stretching from Dalkey Island to the north east to Bray Head and the Wicklow mountains to the south.

The three teenagers chatted as they walked up the pathway, asking questions of each other. The girls told of their immediate situations and that they were originally from Wexford but held back on their history. Frank told them he lived locally and was the youngest of three boys and two girls. He had a job in a factory in Dublin.

As they got higher and the sea came into view, Maria ran ahead to a low stone wall where she could appreciate the full panorama. She thought it was awesome and her heart was full of joy. A great sense of freedom overcame her and she wept openly There was a sense of wonder to be able do as she pleased and to make a life for herself. There was also a great sadness when she recalled the plight of her other three institutionalised sisters.

When Rita caught up to Maria she also succumbed to the emotion of the moment. No words were necessary and the pair clung to each other until they had shed many tears. Frank tactfully strolled on ahead up the hill to give them time together. A few minutes later the girls looked at each other through teary eyes and had a final hug. They held hands and ran up the hill with happy hearts to Frank.

Chapter Thirteen

RELEASED INTO THE WORLD

Kitty was the next to leave a year and a half later, but such was the regime that Lizzie and Lou didn't even know it; nobody told them. Kitty had always been headstrong and now she was determined to make her own way in life. Even though she had been placed in a household in Dublin, she would not be there long. Within four months, like thousands of others, she took the mail boat from Dun Laoghaire and the train to London.

Eight years had passed by now and Lizzie was 14 years old. She and Lou were so young when they first entered that institution, that they scarcely remembered their life before. However, the memory of her mother's death and the weeks that followed were etched in Lizzie's brain. The time had come at 14 to finish her education. At this age the girls would now have to work in the kitchen and laundry until they were 15. She had learned the art of survival and how to avoid various punishments in the first few months. It had served her well through the eight years. That final year was to be the longest in her life.

Lizzie was a bit delicate and that ensured that she escaped heavy chores. She worked in the pantry and dining room, keeping records, cleaning, setting and clearing tables et cetera. All five sisters had grown up there with virtually no contact with each other. They had grown up alone, especially the younger ones who had little memory of their family life. Each one left the institution alone with no knowledge of where their sisters were. They went to work as domestic servants of strangers.

So it was when she reached 15 years of age that she was called to the reverend mother's office. This was the woman dressed in the "holy garb" of the church with a cross of Christ on her neck, the same woman who wore a leather holster at her waist that carried a hardwood punishment stick. Each morning there would be a line of "miscreants", poor unfortunate girls who would get a nasty taste of that stick.

However, even though she went with some apprehension, it turned out to be told of her release and who she would be released to. Strangely, one would imagine that she would feel a huge sense of relief and excitement at this news, but it was not so. Ten years of deprivation, exclusion and separation from her family had taken its toll. She was terrified. The enclosed life had left her totally unprepared for the outside world. Lizzie had no idea what to expect or how to deal with it. She was to travel by train to Dublin with a small bag containing all her possessions. She would be met at the station in Dublin by her new employer.

A year or so later Lou's turn came around and she was released to the home of a bank manager and his wife. She would work for them until they both died nearly 50 years later.

So it was that the five girls were scattered and particularly the younger ones had grown up, not knowing much about each other. Lizzie and Lou had very little recollection of their early family lives and had come to regard their incarceration as 'normal'. They didn't really know the meaning of love and affection because they were unknown emotions.

Chapter Fourteen

SOUTH LONDON - 1950S

The summer of 1954, both Kavey and I left school and at 18, Keith went off to do his national service. This meant that I had the bedroom all to myself, not that this was particularly significant.

Kavey had been looking for a job which would qualify her to be a shorthand typist and eventually a secretary. She was delighted to get a training slot with the Westminster Bank.

I had been applying to various engineering companies for an apprenticeship, which would include part-time day release for further studies to qualify as an engineer. Because of my poor diploma I was unsuccessful. Instead I had to make do with a crap apprenticeship in a crap company and continue studying at night school. However, as always there is usually a chink of brightness. In school there was one subject that I loved and excelled in, that was engineering drawing. Two of the five year apprenticeship would be in the drawing office. I was happy about that.

Before we started our jobs we had some weeks off and Kavey and I set about having some fun. We had grown closer and knocked around a bit together. She was a good sprinter at school and I enjoyed cross country running so we went and joined Mitcham Athletic Club. This was one of the best things we ever did, because it was the basis of our social lives for the next few years. There were a bunch of us of similar age that hung out. After training we would go to a favourite café in Fair Green to stuff our faces and joke and laugh at each other. At weekends we would get a bus or train to the country and ramble through the fields and picnic by a river. Of course we would also date each other sometimes and there was much flirting. They were wonderful and innocent times.

Kavey was a pretty girl and was never short of admirers. We both had dates that were short lived, but she and one of our group, John became a little serious for a while. Even now in our mid-teens, I had the responsibility of bringing her home safe and sound whenever we went out anywhere. Anyway, John had a BSA Bantam, but Dad had banned her from it. Love finds a way, and we conspired a plan. She would ride pillion with him from the track and I would cycle back. When we got close to home, I would take over the Bantam and go for a spin for half an hour and they would kiss and cuddle in the alleyway. Then I would return and Kavey and I would go in the back door. Simple! This went on for ages after we both started our first jobs.

Chapter Fifteen

COMING TOGETHER

A new phase of our lives started after that month and a half of carefree fun. We both started our new jobs. Kavey was excited about hers but I was not so sure about mine. She saw her new life in the bank as a means to making new friends and enjoying a career path.

The next five years for me were a bit gruelling and tough. I was happy that my first department was the drawing office for a six month period. There were only six people in it and I made seven. There was a chief draughtsman plus three other draughtsmen. The other two were tracers, one of which was the chief's girlfriend, who was a stuck-up cow and lorded it over me. As the dogsbody I made the tea, filed drawings and learned to use the ancient blueprint machine. This was a carbon arc monster that required the use of welding goggles. The drawing on tracing paper was inserted with a sheet of print paper on to a vertical curved glass and trapped with a canvas wrap around. The machine was switched on and the brilliant arc between two carbon rods would descend gracefully down the quarter cylinder to expose the drawing. When complete, the arcing would be switched off and the device would be wound up again for the next print. The next stage would be to process the exposed sheet of paper. This was done on a table with a sponge and an evil processing liquid that dried into greasy crystals. I hated that job.

At the same time as starting my apprenticeship, I enrolled into night school. The pattern of my life for the next five years was cast. I am not a person given to regrets, but this is one thing I would reverse given the chance. For me the old saying, 'All work and no play makes Jack a dull boy' took on real meaning. Locked into so much work, night school and study left very little time to expand my horizons or indulge in simple fun. At the time, it was the thing to do to get on in life. It was a total drudge.

The following year, Kavey was sent on an extended training course by the bank. She went with another girl that she was working with, and the two of them became good friends. A couple of weeks after the course Kavey invited her friend, Evelyn around for the weekend. She turned out to be 'my first love'. From the first time I saw her, things went on in my head. I was bowled over, but to say I was inexperienced would be to overstate it. I eventually plucked up courage to ask her out and we lasted for three or four months before she grew tired of me and I got ditched. I was heartbroken and moped about for a while, but like all childish things it passed. The fact that I was going on a holiday to Paris on the back of a motorbike helped a lot. A chap I was working with at the time had a great bike and asked me if I wanted to go. We had a fantastic time and it gave me my first flavour of France. It also awakened in me a desire to travel. This made it even more frustrating being locked into so much work and study, and increased my attention span deficiency.

This was a time that I became passionate about motorcycles. I was given my first motorcycle by an older friend at work. He had a few bikes and had just bought a new BSA Gold Star and was the envy of all his workmates. Amongst his other bikes was a relic that was in decay and he donated it to me. It was a 1933 BSA 250cc which had exposed valves and a gear change on the petrol tank and was a long way past its prime. But it was mine! Mum and Dad were not best pleased when it arrived via the alleyway to the yard outside the back door. Anyway, they allowed me to keep it because they probably believed that it would never be ridden. I couldn't wait to start stripping and renovating it. The chap who gave it to me was very helpful with advice on doing work on the engine. The bike was stripped and scrubbed of as much rust as possible and a pot of black enamel made it brand spanking new to my eyes.

As soon as the paint was dry and I re-assembled everything, it was time to straddle the saddle, advance the ignition, prime the carburettor and jump on the kick starter. It took several enthusiastic pumps with my right leg before it fired into life with some farts and bangs, plus a lot of smoke. I sat with a very smug look and not a little pride listening to the engine settle down into a rhythm. Gran peeped out the back door grinning at me, I loved it. I decided then to take the bike on a major spin the next day.

Sunday morning couldn't come quickly enough and I arose before everyone else. I had the loan of an old helmet and plastic goggles, plus a thick jumper and a windcheater and I wheeled the bike out through the alleyway. I had made sandwiches from a couple of Gran's cold cutlets along with a Tizer bottle of water. There was just enough money for petrol and I set off down the road to Brighton.

I will never know how that old bike brought me to Brighton and back without as much as a murmur. I do know that I will never forget if I live to be a 100 the feeling I felt that day; to be in control of a powerful machine and to feel the engine working through my legs against the petrol tank. To have the wind in my face and being aware of travelling through the air and the tyres on the road. It was all that I imagined.

However, the bike only lasted a couple of weeks. I was riding it down Tooting High Street one day when I noticed some people walking towards me. They stopped and started pointing animatedly at me and the bike. Then I noticed a smell and wisps of smoke coming up at me. A few seconds later I pulled in and had the bike up on its stand, amid billowing acrid smoke. To become the centre of attention in this way wasn't great.

Then as I stood transfixed, a shop owner ran out and threw a bucket of water over the wreck. I had to push it back home with all the rubber insulation burned off the wiring and probably within a whisker of the petrol tank exploding! That was the end of my first bike.

As it happened, a classmate of mine at school, Luke, also ended up doing the same apprenticeship. I suppose that it was inevitable that we gravitated and we became friends for the next five years. His was based on instrument making and production and the drawing office was not in his agenda, so we worked in different departments most of the time. However, we met up frequently and started going out on Friday or Saturday night to the pictures or dancing.

For decades the pub and club scenes have been the centre of attraction for young people to meet people of the opposite sex; not so in our day. It has probably got to do with affluence or the lack of it. There were dance halls everywhere and we tried out the local ones. The town hall had dances and we went for a while but it lacked atmosphere and space. Our favourite ballroom of romance became the Locarno in Streatham, which had both, plus good bands and plenty of talent. We frequented this place for a year or so and had a few dates but because we both were yellow backed cowards in the game of approaching females, we went home most nights on our own. It was fine to scout around and to find a girl you liked the look of but quite another thing altogether to walk across a dance floor, stand in front of her and ask for a dance! It only took one refusal for you to want a big hole to open up and swallow you. Another thing was to watch the girl stand up to be sure she wasn't taller than you. It wasn't good for the ego to be close up waltzing and looking up into her eyes. All in all it was always a testing time unless you hit the jackpot.

So the pattern established itself: work including Saturday mornings; night school; one evening athletics training; Friday night; dancing; Sunday morning training and spending a few hours with friends. At weekends there were always chores around the house which we all shared, and looking back it was a good thing to do. Dad always seemed to have some maintenance job to do and I invariably helped him. The week was pretty much filled up and there wasn't much time left for loafing around.

In the winter months, everything was centred around our kitchen. It was the only room that was really warm and we all did our thing there. Dad and Gran had their own chairs each side of the fire, Mum and us kids would be at our great table.

During the day Gran would have the place to herself and would go shopping and prepare the evening meal for us all. Even though she was only 4ft 10' in height, she was awesome at the shops. She had terrorised the butcher and greengrocer into making sure that she got the best for the least price and usually managed to get a little bit over her rationed allowance. She acquired legendary status with all our extended family and friends, because she was simply the cook supreme. No one has ever surpassed the taste she could impart to any dish.

Up to this stage of our lives Lily didn't feature much because she was so much younger. She was lucky to have a boy and a girl around her age living next door and another a couple of doors away. I remember they were happy around the chicken run and would often go around the garden, each with a hen under an arm, playing out their own dramas. It wasn't until she was 13 or so that she started connecting with us.

Keith was only two years older than me but it seemed more. Being a lot bigger and very popular because of his sporting skills, he didn't hang around with us very much. It wasn't till he returned from his two years in the army that we started seeing him more. However, he didn't stay at home for long. Within months he had moved out and taken a flat in Kensington with a couple of friends. By now I was 18 and had grown and matured a bit. Kavey and I would meet up with Keith at his flat and explore the sophistication of Kensington. Kavey was quite used to it because she was based in the city. Keith would also frequently come down to visit us all at home.

He took up the sport that he started to learn at boarding school in India. Our cousin, Karl was a very good hockey player and played for the first team of a major hockey club in south London. He introduced Keith to the club and it was a defining moment for him. It was to become his life for the next 40 years or so. The club had eight teams so he started at the bottom and really took to it. He rapidly advanced through the ranks and made the first team in record time. He held that for decades and became the club captain. The game and club dominated his leisure time and he remained single until his mid-30s when he met a woman who was also in the club and played for the women's team. That was also a defining point in his life because they married a year later and so his bachelor life came to an end.

I have to rewind back to the time that Keith was discharged from the army. When he first came home, he came with two friends who served with him. To Mum and Dad, he was like a hero returning from war. In truth I think that he had a great time. Apart from the army routine and discipline, he went to places like Sudan, Egypt and Cyprus and thoroughly enjoyed it. Naturally Mum and Dad threw a homecoming party, because they often had parties which all our relatives and friends looked forward to. There was immediate chemistry between Kavey and one of Keith's friends and this became very serious very quickly.

Within a year Kavey was to marry this man who had become the love of her life. He had qualified in commercial art at the Slade College of Art and after the army, was working for a top advertising agency. It appeared to be an exciting job with good prospects. They got a very nice flat to rent and started life full of joy. Kavey was brimming over with enthusiasm and very full of life. They would often come to the house on Sundays for lunch and stay the afternoon. In the summer months others of the extended family and friends would also come and we had many fun-filled afternoons in the back garden. They were very happy days. Of course, after she met him everything else went out of the window and her life centred around him.

Earlier the same year, I met a girl at the Locarno. Actually I had seen her the previous week and our eyes had met, but I hadn't approached her because I was a little gutless. I had thought about her all week waiting for Saturday night in hope. I had told Luke about her and he had taunted me, so we went there with me in hope and him to have a laugh at my expense. I paraded through the throng around the bar and seating areas without success. We got a bottle of beer each and found seats looking at the dancers.

Luke spotted her first; she was dancing with her friend from last week and looked great. She had a pale blue fitting top with small sleeves, a tight skirt just below the knees and high heels made her tall. She also had short red hair and a great slim curvy body. I figured she was about my height with the high heels. She hadn't yet seen me, but I just knew that it would take her to look at me with the right kind of look before I could pluck up the courage to approach her.

She did see me and I thought I got a shade of a smile. The music stopped and the dancers left the floor to melt into the throngs. Luke and I finished our beers and he prodded me into going to look for her. With bats flying around in my stomach, I started my expedition. The crowds were so dense that I couldn't see more than about three deep but my eyes were out on stalks. The lighting was subdued for effect and cigarette smoke hung in the air. Then I spotted them. Her back was to me and her friend was leaning on a column. As she saw me approaching, she became alert and she nudged the red head with a look that said, 'There he is.'

We smiled at each other and with my heart banging inside my ribs, I greeted her and asked if she would dance with me. I will never forget that first dance with her: my right hand in the small of her back, her warm perfume and the softness of her right hand in mine with the great glittering ball flicking spotlights on her hair and face. I was lost for words and wanted the music to play forever, but it didn't.

A little later I saw her dancing with another fellow and my heart sank. I knew then that I had to be bold and take the next step. Towards the end of the night I got the opportunity and asked her to dance again. To my surprise she asked me where I had been for the last hour. That broke the ice for me and I asked her for a date for the following weekend. I was on top of the world when she smilingly agreed.

That week was the longest ever in my life. Everything else was swatted from my mind and I could think of nothing but seeing her again.

The day arrived and I wore my only suit which was a hand-me-down from Keith, but I thought I looked great. I had agreed to meet her at Hyde Park Underground Station and it turned out to be a beautiful sunny spring day. I was at least half an hour early and paced about around the entrance until she emerged. She looked wonderful in a lilac dress with a flared skirt and pumps on her feet and a white cardigan over her shoulder and a beautiful smile on her face as she came up to me and asked,

"Where are we going?"

"Since it's a lovely day, we should go to the zoo," I suggested.

"Yes, why not, I haven't been there before so it'd be nice to go there."

At that point we hadn't even introduced each other and she asked my name. I told her and asked for hers.

She looked as fresh as the air and the sky was in her eyes.

"It's Lizzie," she said.

Chapter Sixteen

CARIBBEAN – PRESENT DAY

Pins and needles in my right arm woke me. A glance at the luminous hands of my watch showed 1.40 am. The reason for pins and needles is that I was shoved into the starboard bulkhead.

Christo was heeling to starboard at 30 degrees and I struggled to get out of the bunk.

"Jack," I shouted.

"Topside," he answered faintly above wind and sea noise.

Clambering into wet weather gear, I grappled my way to the hatch. There was Jack at the helm, grinning at me.

"Is everything ok?" I asked. "Why didn't you call me"?

"No need, we're making a very steady eight knots.

A look at the wind speed instrument showed 30 knots from the east. Jack had the mainsail reefed half way, with a storm jib and the mizzen was down. We were on a close reach into a moderate swell and Christo was happy.

There was another hour to go to my shift so I didn't go back down to my bunk but instead went below and made some cocoa for both of us. There was no rain but no stars meant it was cloudy. I asked Jack if he had a weather update.

"An hour ago it showed force six, gusting up to eight, but it's not that yet. Small chance of steady gales and shifting from east to north east. If it stays like this we will make 100 miles by dawn. Good, eh?"

The nav' lights shed a little light and showed phosphorescence from the breaking sea.

"This is what it's all about, Ads. Here we are, in the black of night. No one within miles and nothing to distract us from Christo and the sea. This is the real buzz."

Christo rode the heaving sea with pure elegance. Jack had her rig perfectly balanced for the conditions and his hands on the mahogany rimmed wheel could feel the sea on the rudder. He would instinctively make the slight adjustments to keep her heading south. Jack took my mug and gestured for me to take the helm.

"I'll check our position and perhaps make a small course correction."

I could feel a slight pressure on the wheel as the rudder naturally tried to straighten. I liked to stand at the wheel especially when Christo was heeling. There was a happy feel to the boat in these conditions. I couldn't help but hope for the weather to stay steady for my four hour shift in the dark. I guess it was inexperience. Jack re-emerged from below.

"Weather is showing steady for now, but it may pick up a bit in a couple of hours. We are about forty five miles west of Nevis and this bearing will bring us alongside Guadeloupe, but about eighty miles west. I'm going to correct to port by fifteen degrees to bring us closer to the island. I'm also going to put her on autopilot, unless you want to handle her." He grinned.

"I think I would, Jack. Don't worry, I will keep a close eye out," I replied and he went below. The course correction required a sail trim and we were now on a beat into the swell.

Jack had developed the ability to snatch sleep whenever he could and also awoke very quickly. He had been down for a couple of hours now and we were steady in the water. With my knee against the wheel and an occasional glance at the compass and instruments, I was free to let my mind wander.

Jack's life and priorities were in the mixing pot. Two months ago, he had made a very painful split with his wife of 40 years. Truth is that it had been coming a long while because of massive incompatibility. However, they shared a religious and moral code and three sons and a daughter, so it took a long, long period of agonising and soul searching. When it came there was much emotion. Their adult children were saddened, but Jack felt a huge relief.

The first glimmer of dawn showed a trace of land on the horizon. I called down to Jack but there was no response.

"Land ahead, Jack."

I could hear movement below and he soon appeared looking disheveled and grumpy. He clambered into the cockpit and looked ahead.

"That's Guadeloupe, Ads, I'm going to find somewhere to drop anchor and we'll have some breakfast. I'm starving."

Jack checked out charts of the western coast of Basse Terre and picked out a small cove which would give us shelter from the north easterlies and a safe anchorage for 24 hours. An hour later we were there and found it deserted except for a large catamaran, flying a French flag. The wooded hills sheltered us from the morning sun, but we busied ourselves tidying up and I went below to prepare a breakfast of eggy toast, tomatoes and a fresh brew of strong Colombian coffee.

An hour or so later, having cleared away breakfast clutter we took it easy on deck. The slapping sound of sea on hull lulled us and we decided to do nothing for a couple of hours till the sun was higher. Jack urged me to continue the story.

Chapter Seventeen

INDIA - 1947

It was early June 1947. Everyone knows that it was a massively momentous time in India. There were only two more months to go before the country would be split into two autonomous nations, India and Pakistan. It would be the cauterisation of a very long festering wound. The clash of two cultures and religions: the Hindus and the Muslims.

The long, long road that the great Mahatma had travelled to achieve independence for his beloved land, was intersected by the path to independence for a new Muslim nation.

No need to cover the much documented historical records of that epochal time on the sub- continent except for me to define this time as pivotal in our own family future.

My father worked for the East India Railway Company. At that time he was 42 and a foreman in the engine maintenance yard in Cawnpore. The EIR provided us with a house in the railway community, not far from the station and maintenance yard.

My mother was much younger, she was 29 and her mother was very much part of our lives. She lived with us. Her husband was a main line train driver, who died of pneumonia only months before I was born. This was not uncommon in the steam engine era, particularly in the monsoon season.

There were four children. My brother was the eldest at 11. I was next at nine. My sisters were seven and two. My brother Keith, sister Kavey and I were in boarding school, many hundreds of miles away and blissfully unaware of events unfolding at home.

The British had built a number of schools in select locations in the Himalayan hill stations. The children would be permanently away from home for nine months, returning for Christmas and back at school for Easter.

They would spend the rest of their school days in boarding school. It was here that Anglo-Indian children would be educated and prepared for life and careers in the state institutions. They were not destined to go on to universities and be the "Captains of Industry", but rather to fill the roles of tradesmen and lower to middle administration.

My school was in a hill station at about 6,000 feet, above the plains of Dehradun. It was on a hilltop and surrounded by temperate forests. The hills to the south fell away to the lowlands, showing a vast panorama, stretching away into the hazy and distant plains.

To the north, stood the massive Himalayas and in favourable places one could glimpse distant snow covered ridges and peaks. At this altitude, the climate was moderate, and while being in a sub-tropical zone the temperatures never got too high. We still got the monsoon, and I particularly remember the rain pounding the roof of the dormitory when all was quiet and we were in our beds.

The continuous thrashing sound was a bit scary and would keep me awake until tiredness took over.

There were four schools segregating the sexes and also the juniors from the seniors. The forest had largely been cleared around the schools and there were well walked paths all around them. The teachers brought us on nature study walks on these paths, especially in the spring, and in the monsoon when the rain stopped. The breathtaking views and sights of the flora left a vivid impression in my young mind, which has not diminished.

Some aspects of the school routine have also remained. The playgrounds of the junior boys' school and the senior boys' school was separated by a "cud". This was a steep, grassy embankment. We would stand at the boundary wall and look down at the older boys and talk to our older brothers, or jeer them without fear of retaliation.

The schools shared a sports field in a wonderful valley surrounded by hills. This was set between the schools and was only a short walk from them all. It was an occasion all ages and brothers and sisters to get together and was an exciting time.

Although it must have been very traumatic for us young children to know we were leaving our homes and parents for nine months, I do not recall that feeling. Perhaps it is nature's way of erasing bad memories. Most of the remaining memories I have of those times are happy ones, and I am grateful for that.

It was a normal day in early June 1947 as I sat in class that our lesson was interrupted by the arrival of the head teacher, Mrs Marks. To my surprise I was asked to accompany her to her office, which I did with a little trepidation. What joy and delight it was to see my grandmother sitting in a chair in the office! After much hugging, the pleasure was nothing compared to the news that she had arrived to take us home. We had only been there a couple of months.

The three of us had been gathered to the gates of the junior girls' school with Gran. We each had a steel trunk, painted black and our names carefully painted on the front in white. We were very excited with the idea of going home so soon but could not absorb the news that the family was to leave India for England. It was a concept that was too adult for us to comprehend. We waited for the small wiry porters to arrive to carry our trunks and accompany us down the gravel-pathed hillside to the place where the bus terminated its journey.

It was only a short journey, but this was India and the sounds of monkeys in the trees reminded us of potential dangers. The odd leopard was rumoured to have been seen. Gran was carried down in a dandy, but we preferred to run and skip along. The bus brought us down the mountain to Dehradun and the train station.

It was a long train journey so Gran had ordered our own cabin with sleeping bunks. We chatted and laughed all the way, happy at the thought of not going back to school, playing with the toys Mrs Marks had given us from her treasure trove trunk.

At stations on the way, Gran would buy food from the many food sellers coming up to the train. She would buy things like vegetables curried and aloo gobi to eat with chapattis and also hot gram and sweet jellabies. After a while we would all sleep which I am sure was a blessing to Gran.

We were unaware of the hectic activity that our mum and dad were involved in. The many things to be arranged and done to prepare for the epic change coming in our lives.

All our possessions had to be sold and disposed of including our beloved Studebaker car. Suitable warm clothing had to be bought for our new lives in a cold climate. Large steel trunks were to be made by local craftsmen for our luggage. They had to make hard decisions about family stuff that had accumulated and we could not bring with us to the new land.

We arrived back home and were greeted with joy but there was something else as well. There was feverish activity going on, most of the packing had been done and we were all whining about not finding our stuff that was either packed or sold. The servants were behaving strangely too. We had a cook and his wife who was our ayah and a jumathar. These people lived in their own quarters beside our house.

Our house was only half a mile from the grand trunk road, which was the main highway running from east to west. It was normally a busy highway with all sorts of traffic including animal drawn carts. But even we children noticed the difference since we last saw it in March.

From the back windows of our house we could see the movement of people like a river. While it was busy before, now there was a constant flood of traffic and people. This was the great exodus of Muslims, all leaving their homes and going to their new promised lands of West Pakistan and East Pakistan, which would later become Bangladesh. All along the grand trunk road they joined it to add to the masses.

At dusk people would settle down beside the road in groups for the night. They would light fires to provide heat and cook what food they had.

That first night we were back at home I remember going up on the flat roof with my brother and we watched the masses of people and many fires. Further back on the other side of the road we could see a very big fire with many people around it. All of a sudden we saw a group of men starting to throw tyres on it. Sparks flew off it and the flames shot up in the air, together with masses of black smoke like huge evil clouds. People started running away and there was much screaming and shouting.

We both jumped and looked at each other in fear as we heard sharp noises like gunfire. The whole scene was very scary and we were very glad that we were on the other side of the road. The next thing we heard was Dad calling us in and when we ran down the stairs, he closed and shuttered the house.

It was a time of massive upheaval with normal, passive citizens caught up on both sides of the divide. Extremists were on the loose and bloodshed and violence were the order of the day. Pent up hatred and jealousies were released. We witnessed a little bit of it but the grown ups were very aware of the dangers to us all.

We were living through historic times. I recall snapshots of those final few days in India. There were people coming to and going from the house. Things were being taken away and also a lot of packing. I remember going away to the jumathar's place and squatting with him while he made roti. He had a small clay stove with a wire grid which burned wood and charcoal. He would tear off half a roti and give it to me even though we were not supposed to eat away from the house. I loved him and his wife who was our ayah. They were very protective of us.

The monsoon season had started, but the weather for those few weeks was hot and dry. The compound around the house was just hard and dusty. Any slight breeze would stir this and sometimes eddies would be created. The windows would be shuttered during the heat of the day and sometimes we would sleep outside, but certainly not during these times of uncertainty and violence.

The compound at the rear fell away gently and ended with some sparse shrubs and trees. There were also a few fruit trees of mango and papaya. The taller trees were also the home of several large fruit bats. I remember seeing them hanging from the upper branches and even though they were big creatures, we were not afraid of them.

Thinking about it all now, it is incredible that my parents and grandmother had no idea what was in store for us in our new lives some weeks ahead. As for us children, it was just a time of upheaval and disruption with no concept of the future.

Finally the day dawned. The servants started bringing all the trunks, cases, boxes et cetera out on to the veranda. We four were dressed up in new clothes and felt very stiff and strange.

A small pick up lorry arrived. All our belongings were loaded and the lorry departed. We were not allowed to wander off anywhere and some neighbours came to wish us goodbye. Reality struck home when a fat Indian man dressed in white with a white turban arrived and was greeted by Dad on the veranda. We watched as they went into the house for a few moments and then emerged. Dad and the man shook hands, smiled at each other and Dad put something into his hand.

We watched in horror as he got into our beloved Studebaker and drove it away. Of course we yelled and protested but the car was gone and Dad had to explain that we could not bring the car across an ocean.

This single event was profound to me and what we were doing took on a whole new meaning. I think I cried then with many mixed emotions and it was probably because it had suddenly gotten serious. I was too young to have any idea what lay ahead.

It wasn't much later that the Studebaker was back. The man was happy to ferry us all to the railway station to start our long journey. Strangely, I have very little memory of the thousand mile train journey across India from Cawnpore to Bombay. However, I was later told that a compartment had been booked for our family as the journey would take some days. I'm sure that there was much mischief and fighting in the confines of the carriage and we were probably a torment to our poor parents and Gran. It was interspersed with station stops and buying food from the station vendors. Much time was also spent at the window, gazing at the varying scenes of countryside and villages.

We had brought bed rolls onto the train and at night these would be unrolled. I'm sure we must have slept very soundly in these makeshift beds. Still after about three days of this, we were all very excited at arriving in Bombay and were dying to see this great ship that was going to bring us across the ocean. A taxi would drive us from the station to the docks where I have an abiding memory.

We stood at the edifice built by the British which symbolised the gateway to India. I gaped at the great archway in awe. It appeared huge to me and beyond it was a sight that I had seen only once before, the ocean.

I couldn't explain with any logic the feeling that swept through me at that time. I couldn't claim to have any understanding of the moment, but something tore at me and left an indelible mark within me that has survived to this day. I was a nine year-old boy who had been born into and grew up in this tight railway community in northern India. All I knew was limited to my experiences of recent years. I felt secure because I was in the heart of my family, but something happened inside my head at that moment. It may have been the contrast between the confines of a railway carriage and where I stood, but I believe it to be more profound. The sight of this massive structure which stretched into the sky and the great ocean beyond, threw a switch inside me at that moment. It was as if it was a portal to another world and a spiritual event that I had no concept of as a boy.

Who can proclaim to understand feelings of spirituality? It is with some humility that I will try to describe mine. From the time that our family started our new lives in England, to this day I have felt there was something missing in my life. It is as if the Indian part of me was shocked and wanted no part of leaving India, while the Anglo part of me was excited and full of anticipation. The Indian part was rejected and fell silent in me. At times it fought and tried to identify but failed. In the early years perhaps, tried too hard

The years have given me an answer and a certainty. The genes I carry are a wonderful concoction. On the one hand the origins are from the cold shores of the British Isles; on the other they are from the deep roots of the Indian subcontinent.

The Indian within me was confused from the start in our new land. It recoiled and tried to hide at the taunts and racism. The Anglo side of me asserted itself and became protective of the Indian part. This was the way for a long time, but maturity and confidence gradually brought the two together and wonderfully made me a whole person again. Some say that I should return to the place of my birth, but I fear that now.

After all the years, I believe the Indian spirit of that nine year-old boy will reside within me forever. Here is a poem I wrote about my life.

Oak Grove and Before

I am from where? I know not.
Most times life takes me, like the autumn leaf
To ponder and dwell is not easy
For fortune and ill have their way.

The complex sinews of social life
Control and dominate.
But tonight, I dream
The past I am denied, emerges.

Long ago, another life maybe
I dream and drift, reality breaks.
The candle flame that flickers, haunts,
The time machine exists!

Images are kindled, I smile,
Blurred childhood memories leap
Then recede and cloud.
How reality dims! How dreams emerge!

How I desire to capture me!
That which was me is lost in space and time
But no...the candle flickers,
The time machine exists!

Drifting...drifting...falling,
Who am I? I am not me,
I yearn to capture that
Which was me eons ago.

The mountain mists and catkins that haunt,
The deepness within me...is me.
I long for the adolescence
In the childhood of my dreams

Chapter Eighteen

INDIA - 1840S

The East India Railway Company was founded at the start of the railway era in the 1840s. As the tracks were laid down and expanded, stations and maintenance yards were built in towns and cities. This, of course, meant an explosion of employment requiring new skills at all levels.

A complex matrix of requirements was being set up and developed. Naturally the means of communication was to be the English language.

Governance, administration, education, training, policing and all the other things necessary to ensure control, were advancing in parallel with new construction and bridge building.

It must truly have been a time of great advancement, not least for the local populations. They were witnessing huge changes to their environment and were becoming part of it to an extent.

This period of colonialism of the British in India, was massive. The possibility of transporting goods and services from anywhere on the sub-continent to the main ports like Bombay, Calcutta, Madras et cetera easily, fast and cheaply, ushered in a new era. Warehousing in the ports also expanded to become holding areas for spices and silks from the East Indies and the orient.

It also coincided with the introduction of steam power in shipping and perhaps the biggest single event connecting Europe to the riches of the Far East: the opening of the Suez Canal.

Transportation times from anywhere in India to the great British ports, were decimated and traffic greatly enhanced.

Towns with stations all along the rail network experienced rapid growth in population and services. The British built new administration buildings, hospitals, schools, and police stations.

There was, however, a conundrum, a difficulty. This massively burgeoning requirement for employees of all types and grades could not be filled by the uneducated masses of local people. If, for no other reason, than language. Hundreds of thousands of British people would be needed, but it was unthinkable to achieve this. Another solution would have to be found.

Lucrative contracts made with professional engineers, architects, doctors, administrators, bankers, lawyers and so on, ensured the very top levels were British and in control of everything. The systems that they put in place were managed by British managers.

So the stage was set to design, build, administer and manage everything. All that was need was the bulk of people to actually do the work. There was an unending supply of unskilled labour in the indigenous population, so that was no problem at all. The problem area was tradesmen, technicians, low and middle administrators.

People to manage the stations and signals. Bookkeepers, train drivers and signalmen, maintenance engineers and fitters. These all had to have a common link: the English language.

Such people were already available and had been increasing in numbers for a century and a half. They were the Anglo-Indians.

The mixing of blood, both in and out of wedlock, had been going on since the British first landed in India as spice traders, and later were joined by soldiers. So it was with the French, Dutch and Portuguese.

As time went on and the number of Anglo Indians grew, they coalesced and intermarried, retaining the English language and names. By the 1840s when this was all kicking off, they were there ready and waiting. It was the perfect solution.

The EIR Company began a building programme of houses for use by their Anglo-Indian employees. These became the nucleus of Anglo- Indian railway communities throughout the rail network in India. Towns like Asansol became hubs in the rail line network, and main roads linking them also progressed, but later.

The British in their wisdom recognised that they had to provide infrastructure for the developing Anglo-Indian communities. Christian churches, primary schools, and later social institutes. These became the focus of most social interaction. Committees were formed by the locals to run all sorts of events.

The town of Asansol is my heritage.

Sometimes I look at myself in the mirror and see an Indian staring back at me. I'm sure I recognise the features around the mouth and nose with Indian genes. As I look and think, I wish I knew something about those genes. In all the branches of my unknown family tree there is the blood of my ancestors, indigenous to India.

Even if I were to make it a great study, I'm sure that I would only uncover a small fraction of it. In all probability there were a lot of illegitimate and unrecorded births generated between British men and Indian women. Going back only three or four generations is quite easy, because it is all Anglo Indian.

Of the four lines radiating back from my grandparents, I will track back on my maternal grandmother's side to her English paternal grandfather.

Chapter Nineteen

FAMILY TREE

It would take a lot of time and patience to try and track every root and branch of my family tree and in truth, the farther I go back the more difficult it would be, especially on the Indian side. Records may be scant or non-existent in some cases.

When I was a boy in England it was my maternal grandmother who liked to reminisce about the good old days in India. She had a wooden rocking chair and she would like me to sit and press her feet in the evenings. She was a dear lady whom we loved very much, and she showered us with affection. It was fascinating to hear her accounts of their life in India and the things that they did. She was born in 1897 in Madras, southern India.

Her grandfather was born in 1846. He was Harry Beardsley, born in Manchester and married to Elizabeth Looker who was born in Warrington, Lancashire. Thomas served an apprenticeship in an engineering workshop and foundry. In those days there was great use of cast iron in bridge building and also commercial buildings. The great bedrock of heavy engineering that had established itself in Manchester and generally in northern England and was to be transferred to the Raj in India.

His was a typical working class background. The family lived in a terraced house and he was the second boy of three. After he served his apprenticeship, he continued in the same company as a patternmaker in the foundry, which employed many hundreds of workers supplying castings to the burgeoning engineering, shipbuilding and other industries.

The house was typical of thousands of others. It was in the middle of a terrace of two up and two down, with the front door on the street, and a small enclosed yard at the rear with a laneway at the rear servicing it.

Harry's father and brothers all worked in the same company doing different jobs. It was at this time that his father contracted a serious respiratory condition, which was commonplace in those days, and was to die of it within two years. His elder brother, James had married the year before the death and had left the family home to live in Liverpool and work in a shipyard.

It was on occasional visits between the brothers that James had told yarns of foreign places and stories that he had heard from travellers out of that great port. It was, of course, a mecca for travel out of England, to all parts of the great British Empire and America. It was on one such trip that Harry made to visit his Brother in Liverpool that was to strike a chord in the young man.

James had taken Harry to his local hostelry after dinner one evening, where they were enjoying fine pints of Triple X stout from Dublin, when they were joined by a stranger to their table. The man was an affable seaman who had just come ashore from a round voyage to India. He had introduced himself as Eric, and Harry was eager to hear stories of the wider world and escape the monotony of his ordered life. After a few more glasses of stout, James got into his stride and told of his experiences in the ports of Bombay and Calcutta. The limits of his experience to the immediate quayside establishments of these two ports did nothing to reduce the colour of his narratives.

He had Harry on the edge of his seat with excitement, with his descriptions of climate, culture shock, different races, food and drink and, of course, the freedom to partake in the underworld. He also passed on what he had learned of the huge developments that were taking place all over the sub-continent. He had spoken to many engineers, surveyors, architects who had travelled on the ships that he had worked on. These men and their families had travelled to India on long term contracts to design and build the vast network of railways, bridges, roads and other great municipal projects.

At that time the voyage was very long and arduous, and took its toll on people and ships but that's another story. The seed had been sown in Harry's fertile brain and the idea quickly took hold. Around this time and also on a visit to Liverpool, he met his future wife, Elizabeth.

It was a sad day when Harry left the family home and his dear mother and younger brother, Samuel to go and live with James in Liverpool. He had managed to obtain a job in the Fairbrass Foundry on Merseyside. Harry and Elizabeth's relationship had developed strongly for the next six months and the pair spent a lot of time with James and his wife. Whenever he could, Harry would befriend anyone who had travelled to India in an effort to learn more about it. Most Sunday afternoons they would stroll on the quays and docks to get the air, and also to look at the ships and cargoes. Sometimes they would meet a friendly officer or crewman and would get invited aboard to look around.

By now, Harry was fired up to go to India. The stories he had heard had been romanticised and he had a longing to escape the cold, smog and boring routine of his life in England. Up to now he had managed to keep his tongue, but he could no longer do so.

On a freezing mid-December morning in 1869 Harry did two things that were momentous. He proposed to Elizabeth and at the same time told her that he planned to bring her to a new life in India. To his joy she readily agreed to both. Harry spent the early months of 1870 investigating the potential for a suitable job and contract for himself.

By April they had set the date of their wedding in August, and the date of their departure to India in September. He had secured a contract with the East India Company. The position was as a foreman in a steel works and foundry in Nagpur, central India. The contract was for five years and renewable on the basis of mutual agreement

Harry and Elizabeth married on the 20th of August in Liverpool Cathedral. They departed from the docks on 18th September 1870. Harry was 24 and Elizabeth two years younger.

Earlier in the year Harry discovered something that he was greatly pleased about. The previous year a very significant feat of engineering had been achieved in the Middle East. A direct link between the Indian Ocean and the Mediterranean Sea had been opened. The Suez Canal would slash weeks of hazardous sailing down to the Cape of Good Hope and up to India.

The vessel was an early wooden three mast schooner with auxiliary steam power. She was a working ship carrying passengers and cargo. The voyage time would be a lot less than going around the Cape but would still be quite long. The ship would make a number of stops at Gibraltar, Mediterranean and Middle Eastern ports before arriving at Bombay.

Harry and Elizabeth were seen off from Liverpool by their families. It was a very sad occasion because it was assumed that they would never return. So it was to be for Harry but not so for Elizabeth. The information to hand is very slight and sketchy from here.

It seems that everything went as smoothly as could be expected initially. The journey to their new home in Nagpur was fraught with difficulty for Elizabeth because of the trauma of her radically new environment and clash of cultures. To be truthful it was a great shock to her system.

Obviously, what she expected was nothing like the reality. The climate alone was unbearable for her especially because of the voluminous clothes that were required to be worn.

The couple had rented a bungalow owned by the East India Company and it went with servants who had their own quarters in the grounds. With the shutters closed, the sun didn't penetrate and the house was relatively cool and ventilated.

As the first days turned into weeks, Harry was getting deeply involved in his new job. He had overcome the initial shock to the system and was now settling in very well into Nagpur. He had slotted in well with other British and Anglo-Indian people at work and the pair was being asked to join in various social activities.

However, Elizabeth was not adjusting well at all. She was staying in the cool of the house, was not receptive to Harry's efforts to encourage her to get involved with the other women and start socialising. There were no domestic chores to take her mind off things because she had a cook, a jumathar and a dhobi.

At least these things would have been a distraction for her but instead she became withdrawn and irritable. Tension between them increased and Harry's initial concern for her and efforts to help her to assimilate tailed off. There appeared to be a crisis looming and neither of them had any idea how to deal with it.

Their plan to start a family as soon as possible was put on hold because she was in no way receptive to him. This, of course, increased the tension significantly. After two months of deterioration Elizabeth had become totally withdrawn and the couple rarely conversed.

Because Harry was socialising alone, the embarrassment of being with couples led him towards the bachelors and that was the road to a solution of sorts.

They would gravitate towards the well established private clubs. Here they could enjoy complete privacy, good food and drink and retire to a room with a young, good looking Indian woman.

At home, Elizabeth had reached a decision. She had come to a country that was so far removed from her expectations that she could not bear the thought of remaining there for a moment longer than necessary.

At first she was very calm about it, having reached her decision. She set about trying to persuade Harry that they should cut their losses and book a passage back to Liverpool as soon as possible.

At first, Harry was delighted to see her back to some semblance of normality and thought that maybe they could discuss things. He had hopes of persuading her to give it a try. After all they were a very long way from England and there was great promise of wealth and good life here in India. He tried to love her and convince her that with their youth, they could create a wonderful life together and raise a family.

It partly worked for a short while but when he persisted with encouraging words she became increasingly agitated and insistent.

Harry loved Elizabeth, but he was now living his dream and while he gave serious thought and consideration to her demands, he was being drawn strongly away from it.

In the foundry he now had a senior position with excellent prospects. The friends he had made were of similar mind and the social life was excellent. He had even been on a couple of wild boar hunts and was learning to become a marksman.

It was a situation of desperation. All meaningful discussion between the two of them had ceased by now. Unknown to Harry, Elizabeth had written a letter to her mother only two weeks after arriving in Nagpur. It was a very emotional one and she had begged her to bring her back to Liverpool. Even at that stage she was certain that Harry would not leave, so she was prepared to abandon the marriage and forsake her love for Harry, so strong was her hatred of this alien land.

So it was that Elizabeth was not shocked to see her brother, John arrive at the bungalow three months after she came to India. She was totally overjoyed, because he had been sent to bring her back home.

That evening when Harry arrived back from the foundry he was stunned to see John on the veranda with Elizabeth. It took a few minutes to figure out what was taking place and then there followed a lengthy period of recrimination, arguing, blame, and all the emotions while he tried to dissuade her from giving up on their fledgling marriage. She did her best to persuade him to return with her, but in the end the die was cast and had been for some time.

John had the good sense to stand well clear and allow the two of them work it out. The next day, Elizabeth packed two trunks with her personal belongings and went with John to a hotel near the station. From there they departed for Bombay.

It would be the last that Harry would see of his beloved Elizabeth, despite promising to keep in touch and perhaps returning a few years later.

Chapter Twenty

INDIA - 1870S

After six months or so Harry accepted that the marriage would never come together unless he gave up on India and returned to Liverpool. This would have been a very hard thing to do and even if he did, he knew that it would forever be a very big thing between them.

He gave up on the bungalow and moved into bachelor quarters. He stopped being remorseful about losing Elizabeth and concentrated on a new life as a single man. So much was new and exciting for the young man. He revelled in the alien climate and coped well in the oven like atmosphere of the foundry. The business was burgeoning and everyone at all levels had to work hard to keep up with the demand.

The top and middle management positions were filled with British men. They also filled key roles on the shop floor which was where Harry was. The supervisors were Anglo Indians who spoke English and also Hindi or Urdu so that they could communicate orders to the workers who were Indian. It was a well tried and solid structure that worked very well. The career path for Harry was a good one and offered wealth and an elevated position in society.

He had developed good friendships with single men and married couples and not all employees of the foundry.

At weekends they would go on picnics to a nearby river and indulge in barbequed meats and curries prepared by the servants. On some of these trips there would also be a boar or deer hunt. The services of a local guide and helpers would be acquired. Any kills would be gutted and cleaned by the helpers and the carcass brought back to the cooks to butcher and distribute.

It was on a weekend trip into Nagpur to a club with a couple of friends that Harry saw a beautiful young Hindu girl. In truth he had not started looking or thinking of other women yet but this one caught his eye. She worked there as a servant and cleaner and was not supposed to look directly at customers, especially if they were white. Harry sat with friends in the fine armchairs in the rather opulent room drinking gin and smoking Turkish cigarettes. They chatted and joked about their lives and jobs. Harry steered them away from questions about Elizabeth and they soon got the message. Whenever possible, his gaze would stray to where the girl was working.

She was quite dark in color and was dressed in a traditional white sari which also covered her head. She was mopping a floor in the corner of the room where there were some large earthenware urns with palm trees in them. He idly watched as he chatted to his friends. She looked up and for an instant caught his gaze with large black beautiful eyes.

Wow, he thought.

Those eyes remained in his thoughts until he could persuade his friends to go there again. It didn't take long!

The social ethos generated by the English community which was also evident in the foundry, seriously frowned on low moral standards especially in relation to racial issues. So it was that Harry was drawn by his heart to meet this young girl, but he dared not mention it to anyone.

This went on for many months and still he would frequent this club, just to get a glimpse of her.

Strangely, although he had written many letters to Elizabeth, he had only received one in response. While he had expressed his continuing love for her and regrets that she could not abide India, she had not returned those sentiments.

He was hurt and thinking that this had all happened too quickly. She seemed to have given up too easily, without a real effort. Did she really love him at all or was it something she didn't think through carefully enough?

The answer came to him in a letter from his brother, James a couple of weeks later. It was a "Dear John" letter of sorts. James had seen Elizabeth on the arm of a man in Liverpool. He did some detective work to get some factual evidence and was horrified to find that it was an ex-boyfriend who she was now with.

So that was it. The news came as a shock to him and for a while he couldn't believe it. The tether that held him firm was gone. Mentally he had joined himself to this woman in love and for life. How could it have been so false? She could not have felt the love for him that he did for her.

These thoughts and many others occupied his mind for several weeks.

He determined that he had made the right decision and he was in the right place. From here on he would look forward and live his life to the full in India.

Chapter Twenty One

RANDHAWA SINGH

Randhawa Singh was an important man. He was a man of standing and influence. A Sikh, he commanded respect from high orders in both Indian and British circles.

Along with other business interests he had been approached to run the prestigious Gentlemen's Club in Nagpur. He saw this as an opportunity to use his influence and expand his contacts and graciously accepted.

One evening Harry was sitting in the lounge enjoying a drink with the local Police Superintendent Bill Lyons, who he had got to know quite well, when Randhawa approached them and asked permission to sit with them.

This would have been a normal thing for Randhawa to do because it was his business to know about people. He was subtly developing a dossier in his head on all members. He had that talent to encourage people to unburden themselves without being aware of it.

He was excellent in the English language and had that wonderful knack of lightening a boring conversation and generating humour and laughter. However, he was adept at not creating an embarrassment for anyone.

Harry got on well with Randhawa and actually learned a great deal about the country, its many complex customs, religions and history. Whenever Harry was there and Randhawa wasn't busy, he would seek him out and they would share the moment. He was also a bachelor and he had become familiar with Harry's situation.

On one such occasion, Randhawa noticed Harry's eye linger on the young servant girl but said nothing. The next time it happened, he told Harry in a subtle way that he would like to help him move on, regarding meeting other women and enjoy himself a bit of course, with the utmost discretion. Harry took the bait.

Two days later, the two men took a rickshaw into a very crowded part of the town that was unfamiliar to Harry. The narrow street was crammed with people, all going about some or other business. The odd cow was being dragged through the throng. The heady smells that pervaded was a mixture of unwashed humanity, dung, spices and cooking all being churned up.

The rickshaw wallah pulled up outside an opening draped with coloured beads. Randhawa jumped out and smiling, beckoned to Harry to follow. Harry had a good idea what this place was and was a bit uncertain whether to follow his loins or head.

It was, of course, a brothel and they walked into a sizeable room with half a dozen armchairs and small tables. There were oil lamps and incense burners aplenty. They were greeted by the madam of the house who obviously knew Randhawa.

However, Randhawa had not brought Harry here just to indulge in sex. He had explained to Harry in the rickshaw that he had arranged for him to meet and learn a bit about the servant girl from the club. The reason for this clandestine meeting was to disguise his intentions, if indeed there were any.

With sweaty palms he made his way behind the madam to a room down a corridor. When the door opened, it revealed the girl in the white sari standing against the far wall. The dingy small room lit by an oil lamp contained a small bed with a thin cotton filled mattress and had a colourful cover over it. A wooden chair stood beside it. She stood with her hands in front and her eyes downcast.

The door closed behind him and he was at a loss at what to do or say. Harry had built up a vision of this stranger. He imagined a delicate person to be treated like fine china. He had been told that she had learned some rudimentary English at the club. After a few seconds of silence, he beckoned to her to sit on the bed and he took the chair.

He discovered that she had been orphaned when she was 10 and that she was now 15 years old. She was living in servant's quarters at the club and had been there for three years. It had been her saviour, because she was living in squalor and poverty in dangerous conditions.

Harry knew then what he had to do. He stood, took the girl's hand in his and placed some money in it. He explained that he had to leave now, but that they would meet again very soon.

On the return journey, Harry told Randhawa that he must take care of this girl and asked what would be proper, and what arrangements were needed to have her come and live with him as a servant on a permanent basis. Randhawa said that he could make any necessary arrangements, but cautioned that she must be seen to be a servant and not residing with him.

Harry moved out of the bachelor quarters and took the bungalow that he had given up. In that way he would have privacy and proper servant's quarters. Randhawa brought the girl with him and he had told her that this would be where she would live and work from now on. Apparently she had no name because she never had any family. She had been found in the slums of Nagpur where she scrounged, begged and survived many rigours and abuse. She had only discovered some kindness since Randhawa had taken her in to work in the club.

By now Harry could understand and speak basic Hindi and could communicate with the girl. He would give her instructions about her duties for the day before going to work. He would also give her some money to go to the market for food to cook the evening meal. Harry had also been thinking about the no name problem and decided to give her a name.

Reality had struck home with Harry after a week and he began to understand the huge gulf in cultures between him and this beautiful young Indian girl. Even though the language barrier had been largely overcome, the way they thought, reacted and behaved was universes apart. He decided to give her a simple English name and hoped she would like it.

She became Eleanor or 'Ellie' for short.

Chapter Twenty Two

The Anglo/Indian Union

It took four months of restraint from Harry and much thinking about the situation he was in, before he was ready to move on. He knew that once he took Ellie into his bed, the social repercussions would be huge and non-reversible. He also wanted to be sure about the feelings he had for her.

It wasn't just about sex. Harry now knew that he wanted to take care of her and respect her as the mother of his children. He wanted her to be the woman of the house and to come home to after a day's work. He thought that he loved her and wanted that feeling to flourish for both of them.

From the start she offered herself to him because she thought that it was required of her. At first she was puzzled that he gently refused to let her into his bed and neither would he enter her living space. So it developed into a proper domestic job and she settled into her duties with what appeared to be happiness and vigour. All the while Harry showed her kindness and consideration and never let her know what was in his head and heart. Of course, Ellie always displayed and felt a natural subservience and behaved as she had been taught at the club. She never came forward or said a word except as a response. When Harry called her to come to him because he wanted to talk to her, she was very nervous and only sat when he insisted. He had a couple of worn leather and teak armchairs, had sat in one and lit a pipe. He had also poured himself a stiff measure of single malt.

She sat on the edge of the chair, wearing a plain white sari and her head covered. Her hands were clasped stiffly and she looked down at the floor, not knowing what to expect. Harry, on the other hand, sat comfortably, cross legged, puffing at his favourite pipe. He had given himself all the time necessary to arrive at his life defining decision.

He started by asking Ellie, "Are you happy working for me?"

At this she looked up with a disarming smile, nodding her head in affirmation and then looked at the ground again, expecting to get her marching orders.

"I'm very happy with your work, you know," Harry said. She looked up again and beamed another smile.

"Look at me," he said as he reached out and took her hand gently in his. As Harry looked at the pretty young face, he noticed that she had difficulty looking him in the eye. He gripped her hand a little and she looked up with black eyes that were forming tears.

Harry took her into his arms and held her close. He could feel her body shake slightly as the tears flowed down her cheeks and they stood like that until the shaking subsided. He edged back and held her shoulders in his outstretched arms. They looked at each other and he knew absolutely that their paths were linked together forever.

Chapter Twenty Three

THE FIRST ANGLO INDIANS

Soon after, Ellie started coming to Harry's bed at night but would not be comfortable to stay there. She would retreat to her own afterwards. It took several months and her first pregnancy before their relationship became sufficiently developed for her to live in the house with him. It would never reach a fully equal status between them in her eyes. Ancient social and class distinctions would always stand between them, and she would always defer to him.

Ellie was attended by a Hindu doctor at home. Their first born was a son and he was named James after Harry's brother. He was the first Anglo-Indian in the Beardsley family line.

Harry really was a very happy man, but he could not hide from the fact of becoming a social pariah. Invitations to houses and social and other functions had all but stopped and he was being shunned by many. By the time the couple had their third child, a girl, Harry was a social outcast amongst his own. The couple started to make friends amongst the Anglo-Indian community. However, it had become a bit painful to have to deal with discrimination at work and he started to think about moving away from Nagpur.

His knowledge and experience were in great demand and he had no trouble in securing a similar position for himself. Even though it was 600 miles away to the south, he was glad to put some distance between himself and Nagpur. It was a major disruption but he was helped largely by his new Anglo-Indian friends who worked on the railways. The family of five made their way by bullock cart and rail to the city of Madras on the south east coast.

His new employers had provided a ground floor flat with a garden as temporary accommodation. When Ellie began her fourth pregnancy, Harry found a nice house suitable for a bigger family. Here they were to have another three children and Ellie would also suffer a number of miscarriages.

The family of seven would find roots in the Anglo-Indian community of Madras. Harry had contact with his countrymen at work but there was no socialising. He had found complete happiness and contentment with his own family and friends in Madras. The children grew up and integrated into Anglo-Indian life at school and community. They all seemed to love their lives in Madras, the tropical countryside and the easy access to wonderful beaches. Growing up for the children was uneventful and they felt as if they belonged here.

The eldest, James, left school and went to work on the railway. He was also the first to marry and raise a family and also preferred to be in one place, so he became a station guard in Madras. He married an Anglo-Indian girl called Elizabeth and they had four sons and two daughters.

However, James was promiscuous and enjoyed alcohol too much. This was the cause of much trouble and misery for Elizabeth

Daisy was the second born.

Chapter Twenty Four

JO'S STORY

A couple of months ago I was sitting in my office chair and looking out at a late autumn scene. It was 8.15 pm, early November and I arrived back last evening in the dark, having spent six days with Jo, my 91 year old mother in Hampshire.

It was a grey morning and quite still. The garden was carpeted in leaves. The beds were untidy with dead and dying plants and flowers. A normal wet and chilly November day. I turned my attention back to the laptop and Picasa. The downloaded images reminded me of the past few days spent with Mum, Kavey and Lily.

She was a great old trouper and the pictures were a testament to her spirit. On the one hand her age and frailty showed up in her dressing gown in her apartment. On the other hand she scrubbed up very well and her old sparkle re-emerged when she had a chance to dress up and go out to meet people. She had always been gregarious and loved occasions and parties. Indeed up to about 30 years ago, she would have been in the thick of arranging and helping out.

Her father, Joseph Clement Vale was an Anglo-Indian and the oldest of 13 children. He was born and reared in Madras, southern India. There is scant information about this time and place but when he was old enough, he decided to travel north to join the East Indian Railway. This was in 1910 and he became a fireman on steam locomotives based in West Bengal. He was a big man and his dominant genes were southern Indian. During his adolescence and teens he had slightly known his future wife because she had lived in the same area.

She was Daisy Mary Beardsley, who had three sisters and three brothers. She was also the granddaughter of Harry Beardsley from Manchester. Her father, James was also on the railway and brought his family to West Bengal before deserting them to their fates. That's another story.

Because Anglo-Indians working for the EIR mainly lived as a community in railway quarters, they knew each other through active socialising. So it was that Joe and Daisy became reacquainted and started dating. They married in 1916 and had their only child on 10th October 1917 in the Eden Hospital, Calcutta. She was named Josephine; 'Phyllis' or 'Jo' as she became to her friends. For the next 30 years, her life followed a pattern that had become normal for most Anglo-Indians, especially those employed by the EIR.

Much of Jo's childhood up to about 10 years was spent in Ondal. Here they established lasting friendships with other Anglo-Indian families and Jo with children of her own age. As an only child she was, of course, spoiled greatly, especially by her father. She especially reminisces about things that children remember.

The period was up to 1927. The world and India seemed a stable and wonderful place for Jo. She enthusiastically involved herself in everything that her rather strict mother allowed, plus occasional deviations from that path. Kite flying had long been a popular pastime and she loved watching the bigger kids make the colourful and shapely kites and all that went with it. The art of flying them and a variety of competitions added excitement.

She attended the railway school and has recalled her favourite classes and activities with affection. Like most people, her memories of that time of her life are a kaleidoscope of good times. Life seems to have a way of removing or diluting the bad and sad things. Going around with friends on scooters or bicycles, getting up to mischief and pranks, are all happy memories to her. Sports days are vivid and parties and dances in the railway institute very special.

The main roads were tarmac but most of the land was made mostly barren by the dry hot weather. This meant dusty bare ground which would provide the material for dust storms when windy. However, at the onset of the summer monsoon period, the land would transform into a quagmire.

Perhaps Jo's very best memories are the holidays. Her father's annual leave was a time that the three of them looked forward to with real enthusiasm. Every year they made preparations for a great train journey. They would board their own compartment on a train in Calcutta and would head south along the eastern seaboard. The journey would take three days and the destination was Madras, 1400 kilometres away.

Both Daisy and Joe had many relatives living there and some of Jo's favourite cousins as well. They would be met by Joe's father or one of his brothers in a horse drawn landau or sometimes in a wagon drawn by two bullocks. Jo especially loved that and it would be the start of three wonderful weeks of excitement and fun.

Apart from the round of parties and social activities, she adored going to the wonderful southern beaches of white sand and rolling surf. She would stand in the water and gulp in the fine ocean spray. Once they had been taken out on a trip by a local fisherman in his outrigger boat from the beach. She thought this the most exciting thing in her whole life. For years she would recount the clear water and the thrill of surmounting breaking waves over hidden coral reefs. All too soon the holiday would come to an end and she would have tearful farewells to endure. The three day return journey would not seem quite so exciting either.

When Jo was 10, Joe's father died following a short illness and two years before that, both grandmothers had died. They no longer had the magnet to draw them on that long journey anymore. In addition another event took place that put an end to those wonderful holidays. It also signalled a major change in her life.

Joe and Daisy had enrolled Jo into a boarding school. The name of the school was Dow Hill, in a place called Kurseong, Darjeeling, which was a hill station in the Himalayas. This was a school of choice for Anglo-Indians living in Bengal. It was for girls only; the boys school was St Josephs at North Point run by the Jesuits.

The significance of this was not only the distance of about 400 kilometres; it meant being away from home for a stretch of nine months. This was really a daunting prospect for poor Jo and probably every other child. Nevertheless, there was also an excitement aspect to it as well, a sense of adventure and camaraderie.

At 10, Jo was very much still a child and loved to play boys games as well. Life was spent outdoors and the kids made their fun in the same way that they did all over the world. Early in March the day arrived that Joe took time off work and he and Daisy and the bearer boarded the train from Ondal to Calcutta. There was a lot of nervousness with them and mostly with Daisy. She was finding it difficult to reconcile the fact that she was sending her only child away for the next nine months. Jo had similar

feelings but they were blunted with other emotions and a certain amount of excitement. It was a relatively short journey and soon the shrill sound of the engines' steam whistle announced their arrival at the platform.

The bearer loaded Jo's luggage on to a trolley and they made their way to the platform where the train to Siliguri would depart from. Jo became aware that her little family group was being joined by many more, heading in the same direction. Before that Jo had seen and greeted several other girls getting off her train. Now her attention was fully focused on meeting and greeting and the next stage of her journey, while the tears were already in Daisy's eyes.

Jo and two friends greeted each other enthusiastically and they claimed their places together in a carriage with some others. Daisy and Joe watched their daughter with anguish as she chatted with her friends. At last, a blast from the whistle and calls from the guards triggered final hugging and much sobbing as reality struck Daisy and Jo. Tears also welled in the big man's eyes as he watched his girls. All too soon they had to get off and join the other parents on the platform. The windows were full of crying and waving girls as the big steam locomotive moved. Couplings clanged as the slack was removed. Rapid and noisy chugging and much hissing of steam as the train edged away from them.

Chapter Twenty Five

JO IN DARJEELING

At the start of the 19th century, little was known about a small town near the borders of Sikkim, Nepal and Bhutan called Darjeeling.

Members of the British Army and the East India Company were becoming familiar with it and its wonderful temperate climate. In 1828, a sanatorium was built there for sick and recovering soldiers. Other facilities followed and a Hill Station was established in 1835.

Tea had been grown in the region before, but the quality was recognised and forest clearing for larger plantations started at around the same time. The whole region was attracting more and more people to work in the plantations. This, of course, encouraged the start up of small businesses and shops.

By the middle of the century, recognition of the benefits of climate brought about the building of boarding schools to the standard of British Public Schools in the Hill Stations, not only in Darjeeling but across the Himalayas. Religious Orders were partners and they operated them.

So it was that the girls got off the Calcutta train at Siliguri and were led to another platform. Amid shrieks of delight and not a little apprehension, they came across the famed Toy Train to Darjeeling. It didn't look big enough to be a real train. A little steam engine facing backwards was at the front and the big man beside it looked too big to fit into the cab. With great laughter and chattering they boarded the small carriages.

Historically, to this day it is probably the only remaining steam engine in active service anywhere. It was granted World Heritage status in 1999. A man called Franklin Prestage formulated the plan for the railway in 1878. The engine was built in Manchester and the entire construction was completed three years later. It was a miracle of design and engineering as the track weaved and looped up the mountainside to avoid cutting tunnels.

The journey would take several hours and would be broken by a couple of stops for the fireman to take on water for the poor little engine. The girls would forever remember that journey and the great sights of rivers, waterfalls, chasms and forests, of villages and swathes of tea plantations. Best of all, towards the journey's end, was the sight of the magnificent distant white capped Himalayas.

The girls were happy to have reached their destination at Kurseong and stretched themselves in the slightly chilly air on the platform. The little train had more work to do. There was more climbing and looping up the mountain before reaching the summit and dropping down a few hundred feet to the journey's end - Darjeeling station.

Chapter Twenty Six

HIMALAYAN BOARDING SCHOOL

"Jo," came a faint, hissed call from the bed beside her.

"What?" she whispered back as she turned in her bed. Jo could just about make out Una's face staring at her.

"It's ok, I saw De Souza go to the toilets." She referred to Mrs De Souza, the dormitory matron. The faint light came from the toilets corridor.

"What's up?"

Jo had been asleep and had no idea what time it was.

"I haven't been able to get to sleep at all. Not since we came to bed. I'm really lonely and I hate it here," Una wailed and Jo could tell she had been crying. The girls knew that they could only whisper for a couple of minutes, until De Souza returned. The big woman was a tyrant and it took little for her to mete out punishment.

They had only been in school for a week and the thought of having to endure nine months there was unbearable for Una. However, Jo could offer very little solace to her friend because she wasn't that happy herself. She dug deep and told her that they would just have to support and work together to adjust to the discipline and homesickness. They reached out and held each other's hand until they heard the matron returning.

Eighty one years later, Jo still remembered that moment with some nostalgia. Those sentiments were echoed throughout the schools in the hill stations for the first few weeks. Busy routines, discipline, challenges and new friends soon filled the big gaps of missing families.

As she became familiar with her new surroundings, she began to appreciate the beauty and grandeur of the school's location. Most days a part of the routine would be a nature study walk. There were many well worn paths around the school grounds and everyone really enjoyed them. This was spring time and the forests were fresh with new growth. There were swathes of rhododendrons, azaleas and many other varieties. Jo mostly remembered the cascades of catkins of birch and other trees hanging over the footpaths. Now the place was sunny and dry and the girls would forget their homesickness and revel in the countryside. Depending on the particular path, they would experience breathtaking views. On the southern walks in open areas, they would see the vast expanse of foothills falling away to the distant plains of Bengal in the haze. On certain paths north of the school, at points, the mass of the Himalaya would be exposed. Here they would stop and gaze at ridges and peaks clad in the white of ice and snow.

It would soon be Easter and there were great expectations of parcels from home. Daisy would prepare a lot of goodies because she knew Jo would be missing her and Joe. The main present would be a very large Easter egg from Firpo's - the famed confectioner in Calcutta. These eggs were great creations of icing and marzipan, with beautiful and colourful patterns and flowers on the outside. They would also be filled with many types of sweets and chocolates.

After Easter and into May, the girls had more or less got into the rhythm of life in boarding school and being away from home. Some adjusted better than others but there was plenty of activity and distraction for all of them. Jo and Una stayed close friends and neither of them took to this life completely. Perhaps if they weren't pals and had friends who had completely adjusted, they may have fared better.

Night time was the worst, especially when sleep would not come easily. There were some girls who really suffered and at times cried out uncontrollably at night. The dormitory matron would sometimes offer comfort and at other times, punishment. This would start with admonishment and if that failed, a spell standing beside the bed on coir matting followed, but usually a bit of a cuddle worked. Any misbehaviour at night was dealt with by slaps, or worse, by having to kneel on the very coarse coir matting until the tender knees nearly bled.

However, there were many memorable activities throughout the nine months and looking back on it, they were character forming and highly beneficial in many ways. There were concerts, sports days in the valley, inter school quizzes and competitions. One of the daily exercises that has a place in Jo's heart is club swinging in the courtyard.

Even though they were over 5,000 feet up and the climate was temperate, they were still in the monsoon zone and this did curtail some outdoor activity. The thunderous drumming on the dormitory roof at night is also unforgettable for Jo.

So time would move on and as it reached December, the time would seem to go more slowly for all the girls. They had started to count the days, and soon the hours before they would leave the school on their long journey home.

Chapter Twenty Seven

JO IN LOVE

Those nine months in Dow Hill had given Jo a whole new slant on life and awakened her to many aspects of human nature. Away from the childhood protection of home and parents, she had been exposed to the influences of many teachers and other girls. She had learned much from the experience, but, of course, it would be many years later that she would look back and appreciate that.

Maturity usually brings with it a perspective on life and so it was with Jo. She never was really happy being away from her beloved parents and home, so there was a perpetual but unsaid wish to put an end to it. After four years, when she came home for the three month break, she made up her mind to plead her case. She was very surprised and delighted to find there would be no battle. Daisy and Joe had also wished for this to happen as Jo was growing up away from them. They wanted her home.

What a glorious Christmas that was. Joe had been transferred to Asansol as a main line driver and they had moved into the railway quarters some months ago. The accommodation was a block of two storey flats. Theirs was on the ground floor, and they had become friendly with the Anderton family living above them. There were two young children, Karl who was four and Cynthia, two. With all the parties and dances going on Jo quickly and happily became a resident babysitter. Many times every day Jo would rejoice with the thought that she would never have to be away from home again. The very thought of having to go through that again sent shivers through her.

Daisy had already met with the principal of the Loreto Convent in Asansol. It was an unusual case but not without precedent. It was normal for railway employees to be transferred from one district to another and so were school changes.

At 14, Jo settled in quickly in school, especially since she knew many of her classmates. She did well enough there and relished the freedom to socialise with friends and to go to dances in the institute which were well chaperoned. Jo particularly liked to go out with two friends on their bicycles. They would meet others and spend times in their favourite places like the small lake called, "the loco tank". This was beside the sports fields which would be used by the schools and would also be the location for an annual fair. These were wonderful occasions.

Of course, by now, Jo and her pals were also showing a decided interest in boys. The pattern as observed everywhere in the world was acted out here too. Often after school, small groups of boys and girls would gravitate towards each other and there would be the normal electricity. However, Daisy wasn't easy going at all and kept Jo on a short leash. She had no intention of exposing her beloved only daughter to fall prey to some "Jack the lad".

Donal Anderton was an Irish engineer and away from home quite a lot. His wife, Betty was in her mid-20s and had seven sisters and a brother. She was fully occupied with her two children and had frequent family visitors. She also loved a good time and dancing, and would not miss out on any opportunity. She was vivacious and great fun to be with. Jo would often visit and loved to babysit the infants.

The following year after her 15th birthday, Jo was looking after Karl and Cynthia as Betty gave birth at home to her third child, a baby girl. A week later they held a big christening party including family, friends and neighbours. There was a big gathering that filled the flat and Jo offered to help out with serving food and drinks. She heard Karl call her name from the other side of the room and went over to see what he wanted. The two kids were sitting on their uncle's lap in an armchair in the corner. He was animated, telling them a story and Karl wanted Jo to hear this bit.

Eric was Betty's only brother and three years older. He was single and when he looked up at Jo, she realised how handsome he was. She had seen him many times before but she had always regarded him as an adult and he treated her like an adolescent. Something happened for both of them at that moment. He was a slim man of medium height with dark wavy hair, chiselled lean features and Jo thought he had a gorgeous smile. Eric saw in Jo a beautiful young woman for the first time. She wore a white chiffon party dress with pink flowers and a pink belt. Her dark curly hair was down to her shoulders and fell around her face as she bent to the children. She blushed as her eyes looked up and caught his for an instant. Eric was captivated and his eyes would seek her out as she flitted about the room.

She wanted nothing more than to do the same but shyness prevented that. Her heart thudded inside her chest, and her thoughts bounded ahead of reason. They both knew that something very special had happened to them that day

From that day onwards, Eric spent an inordinate amount of time visiting his sister and after a while, Betty would comment on it. After some quizzing he eventually confided in her and was very glad to share his pent up feelings. She was stunned and her first reaction was to comment on Jo's tender years and the age difference. He said that they had not spoken to each other about it and asked Betty's advice on how he should proceed. After a while she could see the impact the young woman had made on her brother and promised him that she would help him with that first real contact. They both also knew that Jo's mother was a formidable obstacle to be overcome.

Betty had arranged a celebration for Karl's fifth birthday. It was to be a picnic on the banks of the Damoder River. She had invited her younger sister with her husband and three year-old son as well as some friends. She had also asked Daisy, Joe and Jo. They would travel in four cars loaded with baskets of food, bottles of beer and minerals and rugs to lie on the ground. The river would flood at times during the monsoon and at places where the river would be swift, the banks would be sandy and make the best picnic spots. At these places the river would also be quite shallow and safe.

The men and children put on swimming trunks and took to the welcoming water with gusto, along with much squealing and noise. It was also his platform for Jo's parents to be with and perhaps get to know Eric a little better. It was like a game of chess. They all knew what was going on but let the game play itself out and see what would happen. As the day progressed, the two main players consolidated their feelings for each other and both knew where their hearts lay. They took part in the events of the day, the fun and laughter, but somehow it all seemed to pass by in a mist. Eric and Jo only had eyes and thoughts for each other.

A few months passed by agonisingly slowly for Eric. He was dying to ask Jo's parents for permission to become engaged, but Betty persuaded him to control himself until Daisy was convinced. There were dances and films in the institute where they would meet, but were chaperoned.

After three months, Eric decided that the time had come and he would wait no more. It was with much trepidation that he went to visit Joe and Daisy. Highly nervous and with some formality and without Jo present, he would ask them for her hand in marriage. The diminutive but stocky Daisy sat in her wicker chair on the veranda with big Joe beside her in his, both looking a bit stern. He stood there in front of them and was about to speak when Joe got up and asked,

"Do you want a beer?"

That deflated him and he sat in the offered chair in front of them.

They sat with their drinks while chatting about this and that, but they all knew what the young man was there for. Eventually, in a lull he plucked up courage and he was unable to say his long prepared speech when he got up and opened his mouth.

"I, I, I love Jo and want to marry her." He gulped and stared at Daisy, hoping for the ground to open up. She stared sternly back at him for a few seconds and then she and Joe burst out laughing. Joe got up first and smiling, shook his hand. Daisy came and gave him a hug and a kiss on the cheek.

"We've been expecting this for some time, you know."

Eric felt as if a huge weight he had been carrying around for ages, had been removed and a great sense of joy came over him.

That moment was the beginning of my family.

Chapter Twenty Eight

ERIC AND JO'S WEDDING

Their engagement was celebrated at a ball in the institute. Joe had bought his daughter a new ball gown. It was red georgette and she had matching high heeled shoes. Of course, her beautiful red lips were cast in a permanent smile and she flashed her new diamond ring to all. Eric's entire family was there, and he was in formal black tie. They were toasted amidst great revelry and it continued into the small hours.

Four months after that event Jo celebrated her 17th birthday. By now the couple were to be seen everywhere together. It was October and they were busy making plans and preparations for their wedding. It was to be in the Church of the Sacred Heart, Asansol. The date was set for May 19th. However, Eric's mother had decided to travel to England to spend some time with her eldest daughter who lived in London with her English husband. The voyage was booked for April 10th and could not be changed. So the wedding date was brought forward to March 19th. Daisy and Jo spent a great deal of time together with the tailor (durzee) who would sit on the veranda with his sewing machine. He would make everything for her bottom drawer, from lingerie to household linen. They would travel to Calcutta to choose her wedding dress.

They were a very handsome couple on that day. Eric, Joe, the best man and groomsman were in black tie. Jo and her two bridesmaids were in traditional white and she carried a large bouquet of white roses. The church was bedecked with flowers and filled with guests and well wishers.

Eric's sisters and their families, friends and Jo's cousins and families were all there. They had even travelled from as far away as Madras. The Masonic lodge had been booked for the reception and was bedecked with banners and flowers. The local Anglo-Indian dance band was set up on the stage and the best man did a great job organising and compering. The wedding banquet was a wonderful buffet of a great variety of curries, savoury finger food and many Indian sweets. The pattern was traditional for the time and after the formalities, the party and dancing started and continued well into the night. Children dashed around amid balloons, confetti and poppers.

After the festivities were well under way, the happy couple left for Dhanbad to prepare for their honeymoon. As they waved goodbye, Daisy was inconsolable and Joe did his best to comfort her as she watched her only child depart. Beyond the tears was a great inner happiness. The honeymoon was something that would feature in a modern fairy tale. They had a luxury compartment on the trains that transported them to Dhanbad and along the great plain to the Ganges and the holy Hindu city of Benares, from there through Lucknow, Moradabad and on to Delhi. They went to the great shrine of the Shah Jahan in Agra, where Eric photographed his beautiful young bride in front of the Taj Mahal.

After that they travelled on northwards to Amritsar and visited the Golden fort. They also visited Meerut, Ambala and Lahore and spent quality time in the fabled land of Kashmir. They spent a memorable time there relaxing and allowing the unique atmosphere to enter their bodies and souls.

At the end, the long train journey home would take several days and they continued to enjoy the scenery and stops. They were also busy and content to talk about their immediate future and make plans. They were returning to Dhanbad where Eric had been transferred to before the wedding. He had established a home for them in railway quarters and Jo was now dying to get to know all about her new home.

However, no sooner were they back in early May when Eric got orders of transfer. It was hundreds of miles back in the direction from where they had come! They were going to Moradabad. Jo was very disappointed, especially because she was to be separated from her parents. She was young and found everything a challenge, finding out about her new surroundings and enjoying the love and excitement of sharing her life with Eric. Four months passed and a visit to a doctor confirmed that she was pregnant.

During that time in Moradabad, Jo gave birth to her first child. It was a boy and they called him Keith. The couple was ecstatic and invited friends and family to celebrate the christening. Daisy had stayed with them throughout to help Jo through the pregnancy. The infant who was born with a very fair complexion and white, blond hair, was nicknamed, "snowball" by his doting father. He was only a year old when Eric got word that he was to be transferred back to Dhanbad. Jo couldn't have had nicer news than that, and she got busy preparing for the move and writing letters to family and friends.

Chapter Twenty Nine

INDIA – 14TH FEBRUARY 1938

Eric was happy to be back in familiar territory regarding friends and work colleagues. Jo had friends and family close by and she loved that. Three months later she was pregnant again. It was July and the monsoon season was in full swing. She spent a lot of time in nearby Asansol with Daisy and Joe and they loved playing with their grandson.

In the meantime, Eric's mother who had been living with her eldest daughter in England for the past three years, was returning to India. She had been ill treated by her daughter and family and was desperate to return. Eric arranged for her passage on the liner, RMS Mooltan and she was to live with Eric and Jo for the foreseeable future.

Disaster struck for Daisy and Jo in November 1937. Joe, who was known by all as "the gentle giant", had been driving steam locomotives on passenger trains for many years. One day he had become rain soaked, worked through the day and returned home. He didn't realise at the time that he would pay the ultimate price for neglecting to dry himself off. Soon afterwards, he had got a bad cold and became very sick. This developed rapidly into double pneumonia and he became progressively worse. Within one week he was dead.

The two women were shattered at the loss of a loving husband and father. Jo was now six months pregnant and very close to her dad. She was devastated at her loss and that he would not see her unborn child. The big man was only 48.

In December, one month later, Eric's mother, Hannah arrived back in India and came to their still mourning home. It wasn't long before the grim reaper struck once again. This occurred on a family day out for Hannah and her two daughters and husbands. It's unclear what caused the accident but the end result was, the car they were in veered off the road and turned over. The four younger people suffered only minor injuries, but Hannah fared much worse. She was taken to the Presidency General Hospital in Calcutta and died there from her injuries.

Jo was very close to giving birth. Eric had brought her and Daisy to Asansol to be near family and doctor while he went to Calcutta to the hospital, and to attend his mother's funeral. Jo went into labour in Eric's sister, Betty's flat. She was on her own with Daisy and the family doctor, Doctor Lucas.

On 14th February 1938, with much yelling, pushing and shoving from my mother, I came into the world.

"Yahoo"

Chapter Thirty

FRENCH SOJOURN - 1958

That first date with Lizzie to the zoo was the beginning of our lives together. It was a great day getting to know a bit about each other and occasionally looking at animals.

I found out she was from Ireland, (a country I knew nothing of), and was living with an Irish family in Clapham. She was a shop assistant and she came to London with her best friend, Joan a year before. She had four sisters, three in Dublin and the fourth in London. Her father lived in County Wexford.

I took this information in lightly. My attention was focused on this girl here with me on a beautiful day, walking close together, holding hands and stealing little kisses. I didn't want it to end. It was a great date because it allowed us the opportunity to get to know each other and to either bond or not. Later we stood close together outside her house in Clapham until the last tube train south was long gone.

Eventually the light in the upstairs bedroom window came on and the parted curtain revealed the face of her landlady. Parting from Lizzie was hard but she hurried in and I started my five mile walk home with a happy heart.

During the course of the next few weeks we got to know each other a bit better and, of course, my sisters couldn't wait to meet her. So she spent her first Sunday in our home and was a big hit. Dad loved her straight away and even taught Sparky the budgerigar to say, 'Hello Ginger' every time she came in.

Several things happened that year as well as my developing romance with Lizzie. I really wanted to see France again after my first trip on the back of a motorbike. Throughout my apprenticeship I was earning very little and at this point four years on, it was about four pounds a week! I had always given up half of it for housekeeping, so it had to be a shoestring holiday.

With a one man pup tent made from parachute silk, a borrowed frameless rucksack and a new pair of boots, I took the ferry from Portsmouth to Le Havre. My intention was to walk the route of the River Seine from Rouen to Paris. The feeling of being on an adventure in France was exciting and I relished every minute. Sunshine made the days special right until the end and then the heavens opened. I met many wonderful people who allowed me to camp on their land and some who insisted I join them for their evening meal.

One night, camped beside a path along the river, I was awakened by what sounded like a couple of large dogs growling and sniffing around the tent. It was about three in the morning and with my heart thumping, I groped around for the torch. Then the sound of men laughing and sounding drunk came close. I could hear them talking beside me for what seemed an age, then their footsteps told me they were moving on and a whistle from one sent the dogs after them. I didn't get back to sleep for some time.

It was only 13 years since the end of the war and there was still evidence of it in remote places. There were rusting hulks of military vehicles and I even saw the remains of a tank partly hidden by brambles and vines.

It's surprising the details you take in when moving at ambling speed. If there was something interesting off the road, a small detour usually proved interesting. I took my time and poked my nose in here and there to soak up the atmosphere.

Baguettes, tomatoes, cheese and fruit, formed my diet mostly because it was cheap and I didn't have to cook. The tiny camping gas stove came out occasionally for a fry-up or stew. One day as I left a small village, there was a middle-aged man working on repairing a punctured bicycle tyre. He had the bike upside down on the ground outside a tiny two-storey house at the village edge. It was late afternoon and a hot day as we acknowledged each other with 'bonjour'. He stood up with a grin and said something I didn't understand, but gesticulated at my backpack. I gathered he wanted me to take a rest and gratefully unburdened myself. The man went into the house and returned with a glass of some kind of fruit juice for me. We sat side by side on his garden wall, grinning stupidly at each other and I raised the glass at him in thanks. No sooner was the glass empty when he pulled a pack of Gauloises out of his shirt pocket, shook one out and offered it to me. I had started smoking a short while before that but could only afford roll- ups of Golden Virginia. The Gauloise was lit and the special aroma of it was relished as we tried to make conversation. I found that limited conversation and understanding can be reached by expression and signals. I was able to convey where I was from and where I was going, my age and how long it would take.

He was short, thin and in his 50s. He was a farm worker but had a bad back so was out of work. I tried to tell him that I had to go, but he jumped up and with a 'non, non', he ushered me into the small front room, sat me at a wooden table and disappeared. Shortly afterwards he reappeared with a woman I took to be his wife. She smiled and kissed both cheeks and disappeared. A few minutes later she came in the door with a casserole dish held with a cloth, which she put on the table. Realisation came to me that I was a dinner guest and while the aroma of the food was tempting in the extreme, I was a little embarrassed. My introduction to poulet pot was memorable and the quality of that wonderful French peasant dish has stayed with me.

The dinner stretched and expanded with a carafe of white wine and continued on the wall outside, smoking roll-ups and Gauloises. The three of us laughed at each other's attempts at conversation and got through another carafe of wine. Eventually the wine and dusk took its toll and I pitched my tent in the small space between the wall and house. I slept like the dead and was gone before the sun mounted the horizon.

By the time I approached Paris, I had developed large blisters on both feet from ill fitting new boots and the weather was changing rapidly. By dusk it was raining heavily and I was drenched, but hopeful of finding somewhere dry for the night. Trudging along a tree lined boulevard with nothing hopeful in sight, a deaux chevaux pulled up beside me and an elderly lady smilingly said something in French.

"Je ne comprenez pas," I replied. I had got used to that phrase.

She laughed and said in English, "Get in out of the rain! You'll get very sick."

After a little discussion she said that she was also a visitor to Paris and was staying with friends. However, she promised to drop me off to an area where I would find accommodation. It was wonderful to take the weight off my blistered feet and be out of the rain. We only drove a couple of miles towards the city when I could see a bit of life, cafés and shops. She dropped me off and wished me good luck and I thanked her.

A boulangerie/café was just closing for the night as I approached. A portly man with a striped apron and a suspicious look, shook his head at me as I gestured to go in. Walking away I heard a call and turned to see the man calling me back. He opened the door and ushered me in. At this stage I was wet and cold, and was about to experience the ultimate kindness of the trip. He told me to sit at a table and called through a door, 'Vivienne'. A kind-faced woman came through and smiled at me. I presumed it was his wife. They had about as much English as I had French, which wasn't much.

It didn't take long for them to figure out my story. First I was given a large bowl of hot, milky coffee and a croissant. The wet clothes were really making me cold and induced some shivering. As soon as the coffee was gone I was brought upstairs, given a towel, shown the bathroom and gestured to take a bath. While I was in it the man came in, took all my wet clothes and left a towel and a dressing gown. After that I was brought up another flight of steps into a small attic room with a bed. I couldn't believe my luck but was afraid about what they would charge me in the morning because I had little cash. I barely had enough for my train fare back to the ferry and a bit for food.

I needn't have worried because they just took pity on me and looked after me for two nights, fed me and would take no payment. Maybe I was lucky, but kindness knew no bounds on that trip and I have nothing but affection in my heart for France and the people ever since.

France couldn't hold me any longer now because my newfound love beckoned. Dying to see Lizzie again, I arrived home a little scruffy and limping from very sore feet, but thrilled to see her there with my family.

A week after I returned to work, I was offered a motorbike by Luke. He had also met a girl and needed some money for an engagement ring. This was much more modern and had a modest price tag of £10.00. It was a 1948 BSA with a 500cc single cylinder engine and I grabbed the hand off him. At this stage I was an avid follower of motorcycling news and really wanted to tour Europe once I had finished my apprenticeship. This was the machine to do it on. The Isle of Man TT races and scrambling were the sports of the day and Geoff Duke was my hero. However, the big thing was the power of mobility. I now had the means to go where I liked, when I liked and with the added bonus of bringing someone with me.

Some months before meeting Lizzie, I had bought a clarinet and had been taking lessons. Now I had linked up with some old school friends who had formed a music group consisting of two guitarists and a drummer and when I joined, there were now four of us. We were all beginners, but got together to practice simple classic tunes. We started getting unpaid gigs in social clubs and built up a repertoire of a couple of dozen tunes. At this stage I loved jazz and 1930s swing music, particularly Benny Goodman. We could have developed faster if I wasn't so committed to work and study, but it was great fun while it lasted.

Soon after I met Lizzie, her best friend, Joan had got married and had moved to another part of London, so they didn't see each other much. However, she had a new friend, Violet who was more of a mother figure because she was 15-20 years older. They worked together in Woolworths. She was married to a Ukrainian man, Peter and they also lived in Clapham. We used to meet up now and then and I found Peter had a fascinating background.

Violet had a hearty West Country accent and was from a farming family in Wiltshire. She was in her early 20s when Peter arrived in England. He was interred in a prisoner of war camp near Violet's farm. When the German army overran the Ukraine, young men were drafted into the Wermacht. Peter was only 15 when they destroyed his village, dispersed his family (he never heard from them again) and conscripted him. Two years later he was taken prisoner by the British somewhere in the Balkans and shipped to the POW camp in Wiltshire.

In 1945 when the POWs were repatriated, Peter had nowhere else to go and stayed in England. He was able to get labouring work on the farm and that is how the two met and married soon after. Fast forward 10 years and the couple are living in a flat in Clapham and Violet meets Lizzie. A few months after I met the couple, Lizzie told me that Violet and Peter had obtained new jobs and were leaving Clapham.

A very wealthy couple had advertised for a husband and wife to work as a team: the husband to be a chauffer/gardener and the wife to be a housekeeper/cook. The two had applied for the job and were successful. The house was very large and set in seven acres of formal gardens and surrounded by hilly woodland. It was deep in the stockbroker belt of Oxshott in Surrey. There was an outbuilding with garage space for six cars on the ground floor and an apartment on the upper floor. This would be their accommodation. For the next four years, Lizzie and I were to spend many, many great weekends there with them. The first time would be about a month after they started there. Violet was a great traditional cook and we loved the many tasty meals we had there. Lizzie learned a lot from her.

Peter on the other hand was perhaps the most unconventional and exciting geezer I have ever known. In a way I suppose I saw him as someone I could relate to. He was a loner and totally disinterested in socialising with groups or clubs. Most people think about exciting things to do but balk at actually doing them. He was the opposite and would have a go at anything that interested him. He took up fencing and became very good at it. The woods had many mature Scots pines and we had climbed some of them, attaching ropes to the overhanging branches 20 -30 feet up. We would sword fight like big kids with rapiers and swing from the ropes. Walks through those woods were magic, especially in the autumn, collecting beech, hazel, chestnuts and mushrooms. In the evenings we would roast them in the embers of the fire. He would play the guitar and we would sing. We would also love to play chess.

The owners were sometimes away at weekends and we would visit the big house and play snooker on the full size table. It was in a large oak panelled snooker room. They had four cars: two Armstrong Siddeley saloons, one black and the other powder blue. Both had cream leather upholstery and walnut trim. They weren't seats but armchairs. This was utter luxury. The third was a beautiful three litre Rover. Last but not least was a Ford Anglia which was for Peter and Violet's use. They were absolutely great memories. The other thing about Peter was that he was a big poser. I do believe that given another life he should have been an actor.

He then decided that he would become a pilot. Biggin Hill wasn't far away and they had facilities for pilot training. He joined the flying club there and in due course achieved his goal with a license to fly light aircraft. The atmosphere at the famous Battle of Britain aerodrome was palpable. There were even some preserved and still flying WW II planes, like a Lancaster, a Mustang, a Spitfire and less glamorous aircraft.

After he got his license, I went up with him many times in a Tiger Moth and then in a Bolkow trainer. This was fantastic because I sat beside him in a cockpit with a bubble canopy. It was a modern plane capable of higher speeds and aerobatics. I was introduced to the considerable thrills of figure of eights, loops, tight turns and the ultimate was the stall.

Lizzie and I would share our great times with these friends for some years.

Chapter Thirty One

IRELAND - 1959

After I returned from France, Lizzie and I were sure of our feelings for each other. She moved from the Irish family in Clapham into a bedsit in Balham and we now had a place of privacy to spend time together. This was wonderful and she even cooked meals for us on her single gas ring! Lizzie, I had learned a long time ago and respected that she had a strong moral code and was single minded about it. I put it down to her religious upbringing.

I knew that I was in love with Lizzie and was pretty sure she felt the same. One Thursday evening she asked me to her bedsit for dinner. The room had a single bed which also served as a sofa, a small table with two chairs and in the fireplace was a small gas fire with a single gas ring attached. This was her kitchen! I sat at the table watching as she fried some onion and rashers. When they were well cooked, she removed them from the saucepan. Water was added to the pan along with some potatoes and vegetables and seasoning. In due course, the onion and bacon was added to the pan for a few minutes, and then she served it up. A wonderful rasher stew cooked especially for me in that heady environment made that evening memorable to this day. There was something else that joined the love I felt for Lizzie that night, though I didn't know what it was until very recently. I wanted to share my life with her and to be protective of her.

We sat on the sofa and talked about visiting Ireland and she had lots to say about it and Rita's young family, but my mind had started down a different track and her voice drifted in and out of focus. After a while she noticed that she hadn't got my full attention and gave me a dig with her elbow and asked with a grin,

"Where did you go to?"

I looked at her, then sat bolt upright, looked her straight in the face and said.

"Will you marry me?"

Her reply was unequivocal and positive, if a little delayed and accompanied by slight shock. We hugged and kissed and lay thinking about what we had agreed to. Full understanding of what we had committed ourselves to, lay well down the road of maturity and living. For the moment, our cup was full and the world seemed a beautiful place. We were excited and spent hours absorbing our life changing decision. One thing we decided on was going to visit Ireland. I became very enthusiastic about it as I wanted to meet her father and sisters. We got into the groove on this and decided to go in August for our summer holiday. I couldn't wait for it because it would be my first long journey on the bike. It was before motorways and the planned route was on A roads, north past Birmingham, then across north Wales and on to Anglesey. It was even before vehicle carrying ferries. We caught the mail boat and had to wait in line till all the cargo and cattle had been loaded. It was the old Princess Maud and I don't think stabilisers had been invented when it was built! The sea was rough and it was a nauseas crossing. Though I struggled manfully to resist the inevitable, I conceded defeat and joined the throngs on deck to discharge the contents of my stomach, much to the amusement of Lizzie.

Three and a half hours of that was more than enough and a sight of the Wicklow Mountains on the horizon was very welcome. We waited our turn to disembark and eventually took to the road in Dun Laoghaire and headed towards Killiney, along the coast road. Full of apprehension about meeting Lizzie's family, we rode slowly south, but partly because I was stunned at the beauty of the coastal scenery. We had to stop on the Vico Road, get off the bike and sit on the low stone wall. The sweep of he bay, the foreground of trees falling away to the shore and the Sugar Loaf Mountain and Bray Head in the distance was my first impression of Ireland.

We pulled up outside a small terraced house about a hundred years old. Lizzie got off the back, smiled and gestured for me to park the bike. Before she could knock on the door, it burst open and two small children rushed out followed by Lizzie's sister, Rita. She had her newborn son in her arms and a broad smile on her face. This would be our home for the next 10 days and when Rita's husband, Frank got home from work, we got started on roaming the streets and lanes, hills and harbours of Dun Laoghaire, Dalkey and Killiney. Frank relished the opportunity to expound on the local history and geography of his beloved part of the country. I was just having the best time.

Lizzie and I took time to explore the Wicklow Mountains on the bike and even did some motorbike scrambling on the dunes of Brittas Bay. However, the main point of the trip was as yet not fulfilled. After a week we set off south to Wexford to meet her father.

I was unfamiliar with rural life and trying to anticipate it occupied my mind on the journey. I have to say that what I saw and experienced on that first visit, was a mixture of surprise and pleasure. Surprise at the lack of basic services and facilities, but pleasure at the welcome and hospitality of everyone, plus the sincere curiosity that I had generated.

Drainage, running water and electricity had not yet reached the townland. Transportation services were scant and people generally lived locally as they had always done. It was a Saturday afternoon when we arrived at the cottage. Sean was living with his sister, Kay and her married daughter and children. It was a standard two up, two down cottage on a narrow strip of land bordering the road. There was an outside dry toilet. Water was drawn from a well 100 yards up the road and the land was sown to grow all their vegetable requirements. Dusk to dawn was illuminated by oil lamps and candles. There were benches and stools at the table and a big brick and stone open fireplace. A wood fire would burn in the winter and there was a bellows operated by a cast iron wheel.

Sean and Pat, who was Kay's son-in-law, asked me to walk down to the pub with them. The 15 minute walk brought us to the crossroads and Sinnott's pub. It had been like a second home to Sean and the locals all their lives.

Joe and Jess were still there and it was as if the rest of the world didn't exist. Nothing had changed and for me it was a revelation. I was enthralled by the welcome and the friendliness. There were a dozen or so men in the small room and, of course, they all knew each other intimately.

I was absorbed in the banter and wit, much of it over my head and based on common local knowledge. It would be many years later that I would have a little understanding of the subtleties that intimate knowledge and innuendo created. The standard drink there was large bottles of Guinness but I found that heavy going and took to the Kilkenny brewed Smithwicks ale. The room was exactly as described earlier in this book and totally unchanged.

As I walked back to the cottage with Sean, I plucked up courage to tell him that I had asked Lizzie to marry me. His response was not one that I would have expected from my own father. Sean was a man not given to discussing personal things much and all I got was a grin and a clap on the back. Naturally I took that to be his approval and let out a sigh of relief. That was that. By the end of the day, I thought I had a good understanding of Lizzie's background and extended family but in reality, I hadn't got a clue.

Something had happened to me on that sojourn in Ireland that I was unaware of at the time. The timing on the evolutionary scale and instinct was letting me know it was time to leave the nest. Also the fact that I had been made to feel special, and the atmospherics of Ireland and the people had made their mark. I guess that the die was cast on that trip without me knowing it.

Chapter Thirty Two

LIZZIE AND ME

It was a fantastic year for me and Lizzie. I had completed my apprenticeship before our holiday. We were both about to start new jobs and looked forward to it. I had spent time in the workshops, assembly and test areas, also in the production lines and tool room, and spent the last year in the drawing office. I can honestly say that I walked out of there with my apprenticeship deeds, but without a backwards glance.

Lizzie had got herself a new job in the fashion store, Arding and Hobbs and was loving it. I had been taken on as a junior draughtsman in a highly regarded instrument making company in south east London. I was working with a senior design draughtsman on an instrument to convert optical signals into digital information. It was cutting edge stuff and I loved the challenges. There was another improvement to my life and that was the BSA. Gone was the chore of cycling to work and night school in the wet and cold winter.

It was a year of exciting times, of planning and looking ahead. We set the date of our wedding for August 25th of the following year. Of course many things had to be arranged around that date now and we set about it. The days of free flowing credit and credit cards were decades away and there was no concept of hugely expensive weddings for normal working class people. People saved what they could, family chipped in and arrangements were made with what they could afford. Receptions were normally at home, in church, community or scout halls. My parents suggested we have ours at home and we happily agreed.

A large garden flat was made available for us after the wedding. It was in Ilford, Essex. A friend I was working with was vacating it and had got a job in Essex. He suggested that if I wanted the flat, that maybe I should apply to the same company for a job. Ilford was too far away to stay in my job, so I decided to apply. I was offered the job and accepted it and the flat. So I was set to move away from home after the wedding, but not too far.

That year was full of activity and a lot of fun. Kavey's marriage was in its infancy and they would often come to the house for Sunday lunch. We would also be invited to their flat at times. Oxshott was still a big draw and we would bike it down there for weekends. As the time drew closer, we worked out all the arrangements. One of the biggest decisions we made was the honeymoon. We were going to Innsbruck in Austria on the BSA!

A big disappointment was that Sean couldn't make it over to give his daughter away. She asked Peter to stand in for him.

Lizzie had Lily and her sister, Maria as bridesmaids and Keith was my best man.

Nine days before the wedding I hauled the BSA down the alley into the back yard and put it on the stand. There it would stay for the next seven days. Dad had agreed for me to take over the shed for the week. I intended to strip the bike and overhaul it. The engine and gearbox was removed into the shed. The chain into a tin of white spirit and the wheels were off for examination of bearings and new brake linings to be fitted. The engine really needed a new head assembly, but that was too expensive, so it was stripped and decarbonised. The valves and seats ground in and the whole reassembled. I reckoned that a new head with new piston rings would have given about 20% more power. I could live with reduced power.

That week was feverish and I remember mutterings of concern and worry in our household. Mum, Dad and Gran worried not only that I wouldn't get it done in time, but more about the old BSA to get us there and back in one piece. They needn't have worried; the old girl did it in magnificent style. Apart from having to replace the rear tyre and fit a new clutch rod, she didn't falter.

The big day dawned at last. I had spent the night alone in Lizzie's bedsit. The church was only 200 yards away from the bedsit, so I could walk there to meet up with Keith and the guests. I spent the previous evening and half the night finally coming to the realisation of the enormity of what I was about to do. I wondered while walking the streets and sitting on benches, if I was doing the right thing. Young and inexperienced, giving up spreading my wings and sowing some wild oats, was this madness? Then Lizzie would focus my mind. Seven or eight hours must have gone by with these chaotic mind games before blessed sleep came to the rescue.

Meanwhile, Lizzie and Maria had spent the previous evening and night in the bosom of my family. I'm sure they had a great deal of fun amid the activity and preparations for the wedding and reception. Mr Jenvey from next door had offered to chauffer the bride in his Wolseley. He had welcomed us when we arrived from India and was a great neighbour and family friend.

The wedding was at 12 o'clock and I had several hours to kill until then. I lay on the bed daydreaming and frankly couldn't wait till it was all over and we straddled the bike and headed down the long road. Keith arrived at around 10 and got me up. We had a cup of coffee and he left for the church to check it all out. I left at 11.30 and walked down the road with the sun beating down on me. It was a great day to get married!

A lot of that occasion is a blur and time has dimmed a lot of detail but one thing is still very clear and vivid in my mind. As I stood with Keith at the altar and the organ played to usher in the bride, I waited till she came beside me. I became conscious of this beautiful Irish girl at my side. I could feel her warmth and her perfume left me heady. All else became invisible, all negative thoughts vanished. We looked at each other and my heart was full.

After the ceremony and the gathering outside the church for the photographs, Fred Jenvey drove us back to the house and the reception got under way. There were all the usual formalities: a champagne reception, speeches et cetera but all in the intimacy of our home. It was the very best and we wouldn't have swapped it for anything else. Anyway, it was developing into a party when we left to go and change. The BSA was wheeled around the alley to the street and I loaded two suitcases onto the rear carrier. Everyone came out on to the street to see us off and Mum and Gran were in tears and also a little worried. We hugged and kissed and donned our helmets. I kicked the engine into life and we rode off to Austria.

The first stage was to Dover and it was dusk when we cruised the seafront looking for a likely B&B. There were many such establishments but all displayed "full" signs. Then we came upon one which said "vacancies". Beside it stood a middle-aged woman with a shock of wiry hair dyed crimson, arms crossed and a cigarette hanging out of her mouth. From the pavement I asked,

"Sorry, madam, but do you have a room available for one night?"

Without a change of expression she indicated for us to follow her with a backward move of her head. We looked at each other and grinned, then went up the steps with the suitcases. The woman ushered us into the sitting room which had an old sofa and a few chairs. It also had a lot of boxes and stuff and resembled a storeroom. She looked balefully at us and told us the price which we agreed to. Then we expected to be brought up to a bedroom but instead she pulled an old curtain across half the room and turned the sofa into a bed!

"The bathroom's upstairs," the old woman told us with the cigarette still in the mouth and before we could protest, she was gone.

This was the first night of our honeymoon for God's sake! We stood in the room and started giggling. Well, we would make the most of it and after all it was only for one night. Switching on the light revealed a low power bulb without a shade and we opened up the case with toilet stuff and night gear. Lizzie was apprehensive and switched off the light, then groped around in the suitcase. What she couldn't see was the confetti being showered around the room. The case had been sabotaged by my sisters!

All in all, that first night was a memorable one and not for the usual reason! We got into a bed and could feel the individual coil springs and almost immediately, Lizzie shot out of the bed, ran upstairs and just made the toilet in time. She had diarrhoea. She must have made half a dozen trips in the next couple of hours and then fell asleep, exhausted. Later on we would figure out the cause of it. The next morning we awoke, still tired from lack of sleep, fidgeting and trying to get some comfort from the bedsprings.

As we sat at the kitchen table waiting for boiled eggs and toast, Lizzie sipped at a mug of tea. We both cut the top of our eggs simultaneously only to be thrown back from the stink of rotten eggs! We jumped up and I reluctantly paid the crimson headed witch her dues. We couldn't get out of there fast enough. It was great to get on the bike and head towards the ferry. Oh, we had left the landlady a little legacy. The cases had been emptied of all the confetti as comprehensively as possible around the room! Lizzie was still a little squeamish from the diarrhoea and drank some water while I indulged in bacon and eggs on the ferry. We then went topside to watch the white cliffs disappear and see France appear. We sat on a bench, full of love and anticipation, looking forward to the adventure ahead of us.

We were now in a country which looked and felt different. With the exception of London, it was Lizzie's first time out of Ireland. The day was hot and sunny; we stripped off our heavy weather gear down to t-shirts. Riding down the poplar lined roads of Picardy with the tank between my knees and Lizzie tight to my back, I thought I was in heaven. Our route took us across France through Amiens, Reims and on to the French Swiss border city of Basel. It was our first encounter with the Alps and climbing up to that first pass proved too much for the clutch rod. We were a heavy load for the poor old bike and the last 1,000 feet was just me and the bike. Lizzie and the cases were in a truck.

From the top it was all downhill to the city, so we coasted down and I was very glad that the brakes had been reshod. A very kind couple had put us up for the night while we waited for a new clutch rod and rear tyre. The next day, with the bike sorted out we set off through Switzerland, Liechtenstein and into western Austria.

That evening our destination came into view and we set about finding the block of flats that would be our home for the next ten days. Mrs Schustenhuber, or "Schusty" as she became known, welcomed us with a lovely smile and open arms. She was a plump 60 year-old with a great disposition.

Blessed with wonderful August weather and blue skies, we made the most of our time there. The cable car ride to the top of the ski slopes provided magnificent views of the Western Austrian Alps in the summer. The BSA took us to all the mountain passes and out of the way places. We loved the city and its bars and restaurants, enjoying lots of chilled apfelwein. The time went too quickly as it does when you're having fun. Too soon we hugged and bade farewell to Schusty, setting off down a different route home. We went north into Germany and on through Strasbourg, along the route close to the France/Germany border and into Belgium. That's where the blue skies ended and the heavens opened.

The honeymoon was over and we now relished the start of our lives together and moving into our first home in Ilford. In fact, we were also both starting new jobs, so it was a new slate.

The large Victorian red brick semi was divided into two flats sharing the front door. We had two large rooms at the front with a dining room and small kitchen at the rear. There was an outside toilet. We didn't get to see the flat above which was occupied by an eccentric old woman. Once on a rare occasion that we saw her go out, we sneaked up to see if there was a bathroom and were appalled to see the state of the place. The bath was stacked high with newspapers and the only thing free of junk and in use was the filthy, stained WC.

By now, Mum had been working in the Civil Service as a typist for a few years and before the wedding, she had got Lizzie to apply for a vacancy in her department as a clerical officer. To Lizzie's surprise she had succeeded and was to start immediately after we returned.

I walked through the security gate and up the stairs of a red brick office block at the front of a large industrial complex. I knew this was a business that was heavily involved in research and development of Ministry of Defense projects, so I would be working with very well qualified and experienced people. I was nervous walking into a design office with clever looking chaps at rows of drawing boards. The chief draughtsman welcomed me and assigned me as a junior draughtsman to a squad working on a new and complex project. It was associated with the new strike aircraft being developed for the RAF. I was thrilled to be involved in anything to do with aircraft and this was special.

I lost touch with Luke around that time because he had also married and moved away. So I suppose that it was a time of change for all. For one thing, I was much better off financially and after about six months it was time for the BSA to go. I traded it in for a newer Francis Barnett, but really didn't like it very much. It only lasted for less than a year when I decided it was time to have more than two wheels and a roof over our heads. I suppose that Lizzie influenced me a bit over cosmetic reasons. The Francis Barnett was traded in for a BMW Isetta - a bubble car!

Chapter Thirty Three

LONDON - 1960 TO 1963

That first year of married life for Lizzie and I was a big learning curve. The first real experience of sharing our lives, and the sweet and sour of learning about each other. Although in truth, we were not seeing each other all that much. We were both at work during the day and I was still going to night school three nights a week. That's how we started life together, with most weekends either at our house, or in Oxshott. We were busy, and mostly having a good time, but later in that first year we suffered a big blow.

Lizzie was nearly 16 weeks pregnant and we were going to spend a weekend with the family. On the Saturday she suddenly became very ill and I remember Mum and Gran became very concerned. Doctor Hart was called and he came almost immediately. While he was examining her, she was in a lot of pain and crying. She seemed to be anguished and soon it became clear why. Lizzie suffered a miscarriage. Because the foetus was 16 weeks old, it was well formed. It would have been our first child. A cloud descended on all of us, especially Lizzie. She was emotionally drained and cried frequently. It took some time for her to get back to normal.

It was around this time that the two of us started talking seriously about the possibility of going to live in Ireland. Lizzie never forced the issue at any time. In fact, it was me who was drawn to the land and people. At that time we would go to mass together as would many Irish people living there. After mass there would always be sellers of Irish newspapers outside. I started buying one or two papers each week; at first it was just curiosity and I would check for any vacant positions. The seeds were sown and the idea occupied my mind more frequently.

Things had only just got back to normal after the miscarriage, when the family had another huge shock. Kavey woke up one morning, much earlier than usual and found that John was already up. She got up, put on some slippers and dressing gown and went down to the kitchen to make some coffee. The door was closed and when she opened it, John was lying there face up and she knew immediately that he was dead. It was almost surreal, because she was calm for a short while before reality struck. Kavey knelt down beside John and looking at his ashen face, she whispered to him and asked him what was wrong. It wasn't till she reached out and stroked his cheek that she recoiled from the face that was as cold as the floor she knelt on. Then she came back to the world and screamed her heart out.

A neighbour reacted to the screaming and came to Kavey. She rang the house and told Mum the awful news. Within minutes, Mum, Dad, Lizzie and I squeezed into the bubble car and drove the half hour journey with much apprehension. I have never seen, and hope I never will again, someone so drained of life.

John's mother and sister came over and we waited for the doctor to come and do his job. Mum packed a case and she, Dad and Kavey got a taxi back home. She was like a zombie for the rest of the weekend, but got a grip and insisted on going back to her house to deal with the many things to come. Mum took a couple of days off work to be with her.

It was traumatic for Kavey and not much less for the rest of us. This was a young man who looked great, showed no sign of problems and appeared to have a great career ahead of him. To see life cut off from him so suddenly was shocking.

Kavey never spoke of this but rather kept the subject taboo. Her young mind must have been severely shocked and on reflection, it did have a profound effect on her. She was given unlimited release from her job as PA to a senior executive in an international advertising agency. Kavey threw herself into becoming a nursing assistant for a while.

Nothing was really happening to help her get over her loss and, of course, as close as we were, none of us could really get into her mind. That summer we all planned a holiday in Ireland. Mum, Dad, Gran, Keith and Kavey were to travel by train and mail boat to Dun Laoghaire, while Lizzie, Lily and I were to drive over in the bubble car. It turned out to be a lovely holiday and we wanted the family to experience Ireland themselves.

It was our intention to tell them that we would emigrate there within the year. A month after we got back Lizzie had told me she was pregnant again. This time we decided not to say anything until she was out of the danger zone. I had agonised long and hard about leaving the family. It was a really tough decision, but there was no doubt in my mind about starting a new life in Ireland and raising our family there. Soon after the holiday we were at home for the weekend, having decided to break the news.

After much dithering and mental agonising I blurted it out. In truth we had already told Kavey and Lily and expected them to give us moral support. There was no shock or horror to my great surprise, and I suspected that they had been contemplating this possibility for some time. Nevertheless, this was not good news for them and a kind of gloom descended with nothing much said from anyone. What's more, we hadn't yet told them about the pregnancy! I suppose we should have broken that news then too, but decided to leave that for another day.

Two weeks later we told them that Lizzie was pregnant. It was bitter sweet news, but they hid their sadness well. It was a cruel thing to do to them, I know, but I felt strongly that I wanted our children to be born in Ireland and to grow up there. The baby was due at the end of April so we set the date for leaving at the end of February. There was much to do and arrange between now and then, so we set about it.

Lizzie's sister, Kitty was also pregnant and her first baby was due in February. She wanted to take over our flat in

Ilford so that was easy. We would have all our possessions delivered to a storage depot in Dublin and travel over by air for the first time. Before all that, Christmas was upon us and we were going to spend it with the family.

We woke up on Christmas Eve to a white world. It was snowing and settling fast. We piled our stuff into the bubble car and set off very slowly. In the East End I saw a stationary bus well ahead and started slowing down, but couldn't quite stop in time. The rear of the big red vehicle loomed large and the poor old bubble hit it slowly, but caved in the front bumper. The bus driver must have felt it and came around to see what damage had been caused. When he saw what hit him he looked at us in utter contempt, turned and returned to his cab. We carried on our journey, gingerly. We didn't know it then, but that winter was to be one of the worst in the century. Snow and ice would not be cleared until April!

We all had a splendid Christmas but it was overshadowed by our departure in two months time. All arrangements had been made, but so far I didn't have a job to go to. At that time I discovered that there wasn't much scope for me because Ireland hadn't got much of an industrial base. Still, I persevered with the papers and made a few applications. I even went to Edinburgh for an interview with the Irish Sugar Company. Still I was filled with a sense of adventure and looked forward to the challenge and was very optimistic. If necessary, I would go there without a job and would be better placed to research the job situation, and that's what happened.

The day came and we drove the bubble with our cases to London airport (as it was called then). The family was there to see us off for a very tearful parting. Kavey was going to use the bubble and sell it for me. We were met in Dublin by Bill who was a mechanic friend of Franks. He had a customer car that was having a test run! It was great to get a lift all the way to Rita's house where we would be staying until we could find a flat. She and Frank now had four children. The youngest, a girl, was only a year old. We were renting a bedroom and Frank, Rita and the four children were in the other bedroom. It was all very tight and even though it was difficult, we all got on very well.

I hit it off with Frank and Bill and the three of us would ramble around Killiney and Dalkey a lot. One weekend, while conditions were still freezing, Bill had the use of a Volkswagen and Frank suggested that we drive to Powerscourt for the spin. He said that it must be beautiful to see the waterfall and surroundings with snow. It was, and there were great icicles, 10, 15 feet long hanging off the rocks beside the waterfall. Then there was a bit of bravado from Frank, who suggested that we climb up the extremely steep, rocky side of the waterfall to see what it looked like from the top. I look back and see that as not one of my better decisions in life. It could easily have taken one of our lives that day.

Lizzie had booked herself into the National Maternity Hospital and I had been for a job interview. A subsidiary within the PYE Group was looking for a draughtsman in their research and development laboratory. There were six engineers and a couple of technicians plus four draughtsmen. The company manufactured radio transmitters, communications antennae and radio telephone equipment. The R and D lab was involved in designing test equipment and custom communication equipment. It was interesting and I got the job.

At this time, we had embarked on an adventure. We were young and full of enthusiasm. I was excited about everything and set about everything with vigour, without too much thought about the future. If I had, I might have been more concerned about what I had given up.

The fact that I had come within one final year of study to become a professional engineer. The experience I had started on was leading to a fine career as a design engineer specialising in instrument design.

I had decided that I would continue where I had left off, by completing my studies and finding a similar career in Ireland. However, it was not to be. No such work was available in Ireland at that time. I had found myself in a career cul-de-sac. The job I found was ok, but it was largely electronics and unless I was prepared to start all over again to become an electrical engineer, there was no long term prospect for me there.

We could have moved into our own place, but Lizzie was happy to stay with Rita until our baby was born, so we were there for the best part of six weeks. We probably overstayed our welcome but we were paying rent and it was useful for Frank and Rita. I started work at the beginning of March and there were still mounds of hardened snow and ice around. We were living at the southern end of County Dublin and I had to travel to the extreme north western suburb of Finglas. It took an hour and a half and three buses to get there and back. I really missed the bubble, but it was fine because everything was new and every day taught me something else about the country and its people. I really hit it off with everyone in the lab and found the work interesting and stimulating.

Three weeks into April, Lizzie was very big, the time was approaching fast and all was well. Then a big problem occurred. A long threatened strike by bus employees went ahead and the city ground to a halt. I had no way of getting to work for a couple of days. Then the army was called in and trucks acted as buses from the city centre. I could get to work again. So it was on April 30th that Lizzie went into labour. Rita called the local taxi to bring her into the hospital and she tried unsuccessfully to contact me. It wasn't until I got back home that I heard the news. I was the father of a baby boy! I don't recall now how I got in to the hospital but I did, as quickly as I could.

What a wonderful feeling it was to see Lizzie looking beautiful and holding my son in her arms. She looked a bit washed out having had quite a hard time and I wish that I'd been there but resolved not to miss the next one. Actually, the nurses thought he had jaundice, but when they saw me they realised he didn't. After three days I brought them home. The kids loved having a new baby in the house and spent much time with him.

As if the little house wasn't crowded before, a new baby, pram and all the baby stuff was the straw that broke the camel's back. The very next day, I started looking for a flat in Dun Laoghaire. It was only a couple of weeks later that we went to look at a garden flat in Tivoli Terrace East. It was in the semi basement on one side of a double fronted Victorian house. There was a nice long grassed front garden. The living room was at the front, with a bedroom behind and a small kitchen. The bathroom was shared with an identical flat on the other side of the hall. The house was owned by a lovely elderly lady and we were sold. We were delighted it was vacant, so we could move in straight away.

Chapter Thirty Four

IRELAND - 1963 TO 1970

The day we moved into that garden flat it was really the beginning of our lives as a family. It all really started then, because the first couple of months we lived as part of a large family and socialised with them too. Now we were on our own and began meeting other people, some who are still friends to this day. We both loved Dun Laoghaire and its proximity to the sea and harbour. Summer evenings and weekends saw us walking with the pram around the harbour and me looking longingly at boats. Actually it was a chap I worked with before we left for Ireland who triggered a desire to sail. He was a real tweeds and brogues type and had a beautiful red MGTC. He would often talk about dinghy sailing in Burnham on Crouch, Essex. I liked listening to him and once or twice, Lizzie and I drove there to have a look. I wanted some of that!

There was an Englishman living in the flat opposite and we would bump into each other now and then. He was around our age and was from the midlands. He had also only been in Ireland a matter of months and his name was John. We quickly became friendly and would drop into each other's place. He was building a wooden framed canvas canoe in his front room and planned to make it into a sailing canoe. I was intrigued with this and would often call in to see his progress. He had been in the RAF for a couple of years and based in Scotland for some time. He had learned several skills like sailing and rock climbing. We were introduced to a lovely raven haired Irish girl that he had been dating for a few weeks. Now and then they would join us for a walk down the pier. It was fun.

That summer we had booked to go to England for our summer holiday. At this time Dad had bought a nice little red mini and he came to meet us at the airport. I had promised them faithfully that we would bring Johnny for a holiday every year and would even try to come at Christmas, if possible. I intended to do my best to fulfill that promise. He was the first grandchild and they were overjoyed to have him to themselves for a few weeks.

Little Johnny was a great joy for us and at weekends and summer evenings, we would go for long walks to Killiney, Dalkey, Sandycove and the piers of Dun Laoghaire harbour. I was overjoyed at the opportunity to learn how to sail. The boat was only a canvas canoe with outriggers for stability and a sloop rig. Over the next two years we had immense fun around the harbour and Dublin bay. Often after a sail we would sit on the harbour wall with the sun low in the sky. It was on one such occasion I met Jack for the first time.

It was at that time that Lizzie and I bought our first house. It was a new semi-detached house with a garage. We were to be there for seven years. It was where Johnny grew up and where Lulu was born.

It was also a time of great activity at work and home. I had been elevated to the position of chief draughtsman and was responsible for all mechanical design. At home I took on many things and made bunk beds, sanded and varnished floor boards, play room and sand pit for Johnny.

The biggest project was building a sailing catamaran. It was a 16 foot Yachting world one design boat with a high aspect sloop rig. The boat was built entirely from wood and took me all of 18 months. We named it, "Popeye" and Jack painted the name on the rear beam. It was a really proud day that we brought it to Bray Harbour and launched it for the first time.

Jack and I raced Popeye in Bray Sailing Club for three years before I sold her and built a faster Shearwater catamaran. We brought her to regattas up and down the east coast and to Northern Ireland. It was a time of energy and activity, we partied and had much fun.

Chapter Thirty Five

CARIBBEAN

We sailed from Basseterra on Guadeloupe 24 hours later, having rested, and taken on fresh provisions and water. Our course was dead south, towards Trinidad. It would take us well clear of Martinique and St Lucia, in the hope of finding more wind. It did, however, allow me plenty of time to continue my story.

In truth, I would have ended it long ago, but Jack's obvious enthusiasm and constant questions encouraged me to develop the story more deeply. By now Jack was nut brown and even his balding scalp was peeling. I was several shades darker. While at sea, there was a grime of salt everywhere and every port of call allowed us fresh water to hose every thing down, including ourselves.

We shared a deep respect for the sea and were always aware of the potential dangers. So we were disciplined and all tasks were carried out seriously. Everything was always where it should be. Loose sheets and halyards coiled and ready to operate, and a regular check on the instruments and weather forecasts meant that Jack was always focused.

This long southerly leg took a few days longer than we had anticipated because the winds never picked up. In fact, at times the sails were limp and flapped.

One morning as we were approaching St Vincent, I was coming to the end of my shift at the helm, and Jack was in the galley. The sun had just cleared the horizon to the east on our port side. I could smell the wonderful aroma of coffee being brewed from below, as he came up with two plates of scrambled eggs and buttered toast.

"Ya boyo," I shouted at the sight and smell of food. He grinned.

We began eating without a word being said and then he went below and returned with two steaming mugs of strong, black Colombian coffee.

"Ads, we're running several days behind schedule. I'm not sure that we can make it to Trinidad and sail back to Tortola in your time frame. What do you think?"

"Yeah, it's a pity that I have to meet that timeline for a couple of reasons. Sorry about that. Looking at the map, it is pretty much north west, straight back to the BVI, except we would probably have to make a stop for provisions and water."

We carried on for a bit without talking and then he came to a decision.

"I tell you what. We'll pass St Vincent, which is the capital of the chain of islands and go to the next one which is Bequia. It's only nine miles south of St Vincent and sounds great, even though I've never been there. They speak English and I'll book a berth in Admiralty Bay, as close as I can get to Port Elizabeth, the capital. How does that sound?"

I grinned back at him as he went below to get on the radio. Passing the southern point of St Vincent, we could see the small island dead ahead. An hour later we were close in and passing a headland to port called, Old Fort. This was obviously a defensive position in the colonial days. It certainly overlooked the beautiful sweeping curve of Admiralty Bay. On rounding the point, Port Elizabeth came into view. There were dozens of yachts and cruisers taking up the limited moorings and Jack wondered if we might have to anchor. He needn't have worried, I was at the bow on lookout, when I yelled and pointed at an unoccupied mooring. We had lowered the sails and motored up to the buoy. At the start I was nervous about this operation and had missed one, but now I was well drilled and had no problems. I guess we were a bit lucky to get this mooring because it was getting late and they're usually snapped up by mid-afternoon.

"Good choice, Jack. This place looks great. I bet there's good snorkelling and walks around the island. As well as that, we can shower and put on our best bib and tucker for tonight. What do you think?"

"Yeah, I agree, we'll enjoy a few days shore time here, perhaps circle the island for a good dive site and then make the voyage back. Forget about Trinidad. You ok with that?"

I agreed and we set about the normal clean up at the end of sailing. With that finished, we dived in for a quick swim around Christo and then took the dinghy in to the port. The first thing we had to do was pass through customs and immigration. In addition, we had to pay a cruise tax and deal with the necessary paperwork. With that done and over with, it was just great to stroll at our ease. We stopped at a beach bar and had a beer, before checking out some restaurant menus for later on.

We walked on and took the street that wound up a hill behind the town. There were the usual shanty type houses colourfully painted, and scattered here and there. A couple of hundred yards further up we saw a restaurant with an open balcony facing the bay. It was called, "Aunty Josie's".

We walked straight in and booked a table for eight o'clock. What a view and we hoped the food and atmosphere would match it. We hadn't treated ourselves for weeks and couldn't wait. Back on Christo we lounged, downed a couple of vodkas and watched the sun go down.

After showering and getting dressed, we lowered ourselves into the dinghy, wearing chino's, polo shirts and flip flops. The Yamaha hummed and weaved us easily through the moored boats to a jetty already full of dinghy's but we managed to squeeze in. I loved the sight of these places at the time. The sky was not yet fully dark but deep blue and only the brightest stars showed. Lights from the waterfront and boats twinkling and reflecting in the water, is magical.

"How about a nice cold margarita, Ads?"

"You're on my wavelength. Let's try that bar we spotted earlier."

It was still only seven o'clock so there was plenty of time. The waterfront was quite busy, but no one seemed in any particular hurry. The bar overlooked the harbour and was jointed. We were lucky to get seats. It was manned by a middle- aged Rastafarian and his woman, mostly with people like us from boats. Bob Marley was belting it out from an old turntable. We knocked back three wonderful cold margaritas before it was time to take the walk up the hill. The alcohol had done its work and we fooled around going up.

Aunty Josie turned out to be a well endowed lady and around 45 or so. Her Dublin accent was unsullied and she greeted us with gusto. Jack was delighted to get a big hug. She guided us over to a table with an uninterrupted view at the outside corner of the terrace. I looked at Jack, who was preoccupied with the Dame de Maison. A light kick under the table got his attention.

"Fancy your chances? You haven't got a prayer," I goaded him.

"Ten says you take the dink back to Christo on your own," he countered.

We laughed as I caught her eye for two margaritas. There were eight tables on the terrace and a further half dozen inside. Three tables including ours, were occupied and then two couples were shown to the table beside us. They were a generation younger than us and good looking people. True to form, Jack struck up conversation immediately after an exchange of greetings. Half standing, with a wicked grin, he doffed his cap, revealing his thinning hair.

"Dear ladies, if you should find your male companions tiresome and wish to greatly enhance your evening with wit and amazing repartee, look no further. As you can see we," He gestured towards me, "are exceedingly handsome fellows and our wealth of experience and maturity will stun you. These chaps with you are no match for us."

With that he half bowed, grinning and sat down. Of course, that generated a great laugh and set the stage for the evening. They were from Boston and had chartered a Sunseeker 36. This was their second night in a row in Josie's.

I leaned back in the creaking wicker chair
and looked out at the sub-tropical scene below us. Lights from the beach area and boats shone on a calm night scene. The still frosted glass of margherita still had some magic in it and it disappeared in one. Jack and I slipped into a short period of silence and contemplation which was only broken when our main courses arrived. We had both ordered grilled Dorado steaks with green salad and French fries. The food didn't last long as we were very ravenous.

By the time we had to stagger boisterously down to the beach with our new found friends, it was the early hours. They turned out to be great fun and, of course, this was tremendous encouragement for Jack to dig deep into his repertoire of wit. We were the last and Josie had joined us on the veranda to start us singing with her wonderful voice

Chapter Thirty Six

NOWADAYS AND REFLECTIONS PART 1

A couple of years ago we bought an apartment in Vera, south east Spain. It's a semi-desert there and is a stark contrast to Cork. A quarter of our lives are spent there now. It was October and Lizzie and I had just returned to find the large gravel areas around the house carpeted with ash, birch, alder and acer leaves.

One morning I went out to our garden, 15 degrees colder than Vera, but the weather was fine. I got the blower out and cleared leaves from the gravel. Then I placed the ladder against the damson tree and collected a bag of beautiful black fruits, soft and ripe. After climbing down the ladder, I sat on the bench and looked at the scene around me. The high wall was ablaze with the red of Virginia creeper and a lot of multicolour nasturtiums. The ash behind me had already taken on a bare winter look, while its neighbouring birch was sparse and yellow.

The sparrows, greenfinches, chaffinches, great tits, blue tits, coal tits and occasional bull finches, are a constant and their sight and sound added great life to the scene.

Later we jumped into the car and headed for Henchy's Pub in St Lukes, Cork. Johnny had a couple of pieces on show at a charity art exhibition. They also featured a "stew competition". He entered his own beef stew and Lizzie entered her amazing Irish stew. It was a bit of fun, as Lulu and Joey would be there too.

There was a great mix of paintings in Henchy's, mostly of Cork artists along with some amateur works. Johnny's "Triptych of the Docklands" had pride of place and was the most expensive painting. He had shown three others and sold one. The pub has two main areas in the front plus five smaller areas at the rear. It is a rambling place and the atmosphere was ideal for this event.

We arrived early enough to claim a table for six in one of the rear rooms. The sixth person was a rather attractive young lady who very definitely had zoned in on Johnny. However, he was not zoned in on her. We were introduced to Helen. His German casual girlfriend arrived. He is a very gregarious chap and this is his "village". He seemed to know everyone.

An hour later the place was buzzing and heaving. People squeezed past each other like fish in a net.

A rather portly guy arrived at the table and engaged John in conversation. We learned that he's in the music business and is a singer. It appeared that John played drums in a band he sings with. He was a funny guy and soon we were all chuckling and laughing. He brought John off with him to meet someone. Helen looked glum and began to get the message.

A couple of hours passed and the intake of alcohol started to show as people began to get animated and loosen up for the night. Lulu was enjoying herself and stayed with Johnny and a few friends for the evening. After a glance at Lizzie, I went looking for Joey. A few minutes later we treaded through the throng and exited to a beautiful, crisp clear night. Many people were on the sidewalk drinking and smoking as we headed to our car.

Chapter Thirty Seven

NOWADAYS AND REFLECTIONS PART 2

Many years ago in a different place I made a large pine kitchen table and a settee for our young family. These now dominate my small office at home. I sit at a compact leather office swivel chair and the only other items are a small wooden filing cabinet, and a sofa that I also made at that time.

The walls are covered with a myriad assortment of memorabilia from old photos, posters of Johnny's last art exhibition, my mother when she was 17, a wall planner showing important dates for the year. The wall in front of me has a large framed parchment chart of the Virgin Islands. It always brings back wonderful memories of times with Jack and Christo.

Only a couple of hours each day are spent working on my laptop these days. The design consultancy I started years ago has passed on to our daughter, Lulu. The room is at the front of the cottage and I have a full view of our large and beautiful garden. At this time of year, the white blooms of a Japanese anemone at the window, nod their heads at me in the breeze. In the background, the garden is trim and a fascinating display of colour. It is a joyful place for us.

The pressures and commitments of earlier years have departed, leaving me with the luxury and opportunity to indulge some time in rumination and other useless things. As well as being philosophical about our current lifestyle, current affairs and other worldly things, which I suppose is mandatory for an old fart, my thoughts nearly always drift back to my origins and early life.

Fifty years together have fused the individual lives of Lizzie and I. While we do enjoy some separate activities which fulfil our different personalities, it is not possible to imagine separate lives. We are most fortunate to have love and contentment, and freedom to choose our path together.

At this moment my thoughts are with Johnny. He is with his friend on a yacht, cruising the Atlantic waters of West Cork. Our concern is that they are safe and well, and hopefully enjoying good sailing weather. He is a painter and has the spirit of a true artist. Johnny doesn't possess the skills of a technician, but instead the excitement of boldness and experimentation. Rich and unique canvasses of colour and composition and often applied to land and seascapes. He is our first born.

It had been quite a wet summer so far as we headed towards autumn. In fact, some towns in the north of the county suffered serious flooding and farmers were worried about the harvest. But the sun came out that morning as I looked out at the garden. I took the opportunity to go out with my little Pentax and photographed the early August blooms. I try to record the garden at the start of each month. This technology enables me to review and enjoy the very different colours, textures and light of the seasons. It is a pleasure.

Every species of local finch and tit occupy the garden. This is because Lizzie spends a lot of time and money on feeding them. Many branches are festooned with feeders and she has devised ways to ensure that larger birds can't access them.

Lulu took her son to Allihies for the weekend with some friends. Joey is twelve and had been away for a week of outdoor activities in Rockwell. They came home earlier in the day and Lulu had a mass of Joey's dirty clothes to deal with. They will also reunite with Georgy, who had been in kennels for some days.

The previous morning as I sat checking my emails, I heard a dull thump from the bedroom. I immediately knew what it was but puzzled as to what caused it. Green tits regularly bang into the windows and sometimes die, but the sound this morning was from something bigger. I went to the front porch and looked to my right. There, spread eagled under the window, was a Sparrowhawk. He lay on his belly with wings spread out, his head up and his sharp bright but dazed eyes stared straight at me. We were both surprised at seeing each other. I managed to take two steps toward him before he gathered his wits and flew away into the trees.

Thank God he wasn't injured. But there beside where he lay, was another bundle of feathers, but this time lying still and inert, a collared dove. Twenty feet away on the lawn some pale grey feathers told the story. The hawk struck the unfortunate dove there on the wing and carried it straight into the window. This acted as a reminder that to the eye, a garden is a place of peace and tranquillity; not so for the creatures that inhabit it. It is a savage world of survival.

Lizzie was busy preparing for our trip to England that afternoon. Johnny, Joey, Lizzie and I were going to spend a week at my sister's cottage in Godalming. We were also going to see my mother who was ninety one this year.

Chapter Thirty Eight

OCTOBER 2009

Lizzie and I travelled to Hampshire to celebrate Kavey's 70th birthday on July 26th. We stayed with Bootsie and Lily for the five days and Jo was there too. After that we were booked to fly to New York for a week and then on to Connecticut for another week. It was also Jack's 70th birthday and we were very happy to be with him for that.

Jo had deteriorated significantly in the couple of months since we last saw her. She struggled to move around at all now and even a short walk to the bathroom left her breathless and exhausted. Her short term memory was non-existent, but she could still beat off all comers at scrabble and have a laugh. What a mum!

The weather was a bonus and we enjoyed those few days together before going down to Kavey's celebrations. There was no wild party or anything. Her kids had booked the local Indian restaurant for 16 of us and after in her house. It was very pleasant. The day we were leaving for the USA I did feel a slight reluctance to be saying goodbye to Mum, but promised to be back in October for her 92nd birthday.

New York was a first for me and Lizzie. It was a revelation and we walked our feet off. Our base was Fitzpatricks Hotel in mid-town Manhattan, and it turned out to be very central. Of course, a week there only made it possible to get a flavour of the mighty city. Lizzie enjoyed shopping at Bloomingdales and Macys, while I spent half a day in the Museum of Modern Art.

Our walks together were the best, finding places like Madison Square Garden and Central Park. I stood in awe outside the brownstone Carnegie Hall, where my favourite concert of all time was performed. The year I was born, Benny Goodman and his band, along with most of the top jazz greats, jammed it up in that building. We looked down on the city from the top of the Empire State Building and marvelled at the eccentricity and beauty of the Art Nouveau Chrysler Building.

We felt a real sense of the horror that was perpetrated on the city and its citizens as we stood at ground zero. Sitting in St Patricks Cathedral, after close up views of the Statue of Liberty and Ellis Island, brought alive feelings of history and connection. Irish emigrants, fleeing the ravages of starvation and famine 160 years before, would have left their land looking back at that great Cathedral on the hill overlooking Cork Harbour. The ones who survived that journey and settled in New York would have sat in those pews and perhaps remembered that last sight of their homeland.

I guess that Manhattan itself left us with a feeling of massive power and wealth. We were here in the heartland of capitalism and there was no sign at all of a recession. Things happened here and decisions made that shaped much of the world. Everything here is outsize and we were in awe, but at the same time felt welcome. Perhaps if we had visited other suburban parts of the city, we would have seen the flip side of the coin.

On the last day we got a yellow cab to Penn Station and got on a train to Old Saybrook in Connecticut. It was enjoyable and relaxing, after the buzz of the Metropolis. The view of Manhattan and the bridges from a distance re-focused the scale. It was now a small irregularity on the skyline and not all that significant to the landmass. We chatted and reminisced about the past week as the changing scenery slid by.

A diminutive but young looking white haired woman sitting across from us looked over and smiled, which encouraged us to enter into conversation. The topics ranged from food to travel and painting to families. It turned out that she was on her way to celebrate her grandson's 21st birthday in Boston. We had discovered she was a seasoned traveller and lover of the arts. Apparently her husband was a well known American artist. She was about 15 years older than she looked and her husband two years older at 82. The real punch line came when she said he was in Patagonia climbing one of South America's highest peaks, and in a week she was flying out to join him! We were gobsmacked, a chance encounter revealed a remarkable woman.

It was 25 degrees as we stood outside the red brick station waiting for Jack. A couple of minutes later, a silver grey Honda Element squealed around the corner and there he was with his arm out of the window, waving. Loving greetings, hugs and kisses followed and we were soon barrelling down the road. I looked at Lizzie and smiled. This was Jack, never hanging around, always hectic action. Questions and answers sprang from each of us and very soon he turned off the narrow, twisty wooded road into a curving driveway. This opened up to an expansive garden and revealed a very large, sprawling white and grey clapboard house. Everything we saw then and subsequently of the house, gardens, and views had what is now commonly referred to as the "wow" factor.

Once inside we were introduced to a good looking woman who he now shared his life with. Having had a tour of house and gardens, we relaxed beside the pool, sipping cold drinks, sharing news and catching up. Jack's sister and husband were there too and we celebrated his birthday that first night with a great meal al fresco.

We had full use of the Honda while we were there and the four of us spent the days investigating that part of Connecticut. The next day was his birthday and the real celebration was that night. There were 15 of us to dinner at a beach club, again al fresco. Jack's three sons and daughter with their respective partners made it a really lively time and we all enjoyed it hugely.

The next night was another celebration in the beautiful grounds of a local gallery/museum. A large open sided marquee was set up for the summer and a variety of events happened there. This night was the annual samba party. A large deck was the dance area in the middle and a 15 piece Brazilian band provided the pulsing rhythm. There was a scantily clad beauty dancing and providing lessons to the gyrating tryers. Clever lighting and many lanterns created an exciting atmosphere. From there, the lawns sloped downhill towards mature trees and a reeds banked river. A wonderful sunset completed the scene.

We filled the days of the short week and on the final morning, we all descended on a favourite café in Essex for breakfast.

Jack drove us to the Connecticut limo base for our ride to JFK and we said our goodbyes with promises to see each other as soon as possible.

It was mid August and as we relaxed in the Virgin Atlantic Jumbo, we had no idea of what lay ahead.

Chapter Thirty Nine

TWIN SHOCKS

Being an infrequent traveller across the Atlantic, I didn't pay attention to the different time zones! I had scheduled to travel from Heathrow to Cork on the same day as we left New York. When we went to the check-in desk I discovered my error. I now had to make a new booking in two days time. Lily and Bootsie came to the rescue and we spent the next few days with them.

It was an unexpected bonus as Jo was there as well. It was great to spend a few more days with her again, though she was very frail and was unable to walk without getting breathless. Still we shared our experiences in the USA and downloaded the hundreds of digital images I had taken. She was excited by the images of Manhattan and loved to see Jack who she had not seen for a long time. This unexpected time with Mum was truly fateful, although we did not know it then.

The two days passed quickly and we arrived back in Cork. It's always good to get home and we immediately began tidying up the garden and Lizzie was happy to play some golf again. We had missed spending time with our family and enjoyed that very much.

Four weeks later we were asleep when the phone rang at around 1.00 pm. It was Lily, clearly very upset and crying. Mum was there with them again for a few days while Kavey was away. These days Lily slept with her in a double bed in case of emergency during the night. She had suddenly woken in a very distressed and incoherent state. Bootsie had called an ambulance which arrived promptly and had taken her to the hospital. They were heading there now and would ring again with news. Something told me that she wasn't going to survive this one and we waited for the call. It came about an hour later.

We phoned Johnny and Lulu and waited for the call we dreaded. Sleep was out of the question now, so I went to the laptop and booked flights for us all. It was time to get together with the family. Unfortunately Kavey was in Chicago and would have to cut her holiday short.

Jo was the last of her generation in the family and enjoyed huge popularity and love. People came from far and wide for the funeral service and there were many touching words from the grandchildren. With the passage of time, the sadness has softened and we now celebrate her 92 years of life. Personally I believe that she gifted me with much from the beauty of her personality and humanity and I will remember her with much love for each day of my life. Two weeks later it would have been her 92nd birthday. Kavey and Lily were going to spend the day in Mum's apartment and I asked them to pin the following words on the wall for the day:

10th October 2009

Happy Birthday Mum,

I wish I was there and I wish that you were there to give each other big hugs and kisses. Your centre of gravity has gone and there is a gaping hole in our lives. It will take some time while we wander hither and thither trying to fill the gap. Somehow you managed to share yourself with each of your four children and completely did it without fear or favour. That is one lesson you taught me among many.

It's dawn here in Cork. The sky is lightening and streaked with pink cirrus. There is mist and it's very chilly. Ninety two years ago on this day, you entered this world in a very different place. Deep in thought about you, I see to my left a beautiful slip of a girl of 16 standing amongst flower pots. On the windowsill is a picture of you and me, sitting at Lily's table chatting and joking as we did.

Happy Birthday Mum,

In many ways, in my eyes, you live on. I see you in our children, your grandchildren. They have inherited many of your characteristics. Perhaps from now on, I will look at them more closely with that in mind. You see, grief and sadness at your passing are transforming into something else. This message to you has been from me, but now it's time to tell you that we, as your family in Ireland will treasure your memory and celebrate your long life from now on for always.

***

Exactly one month after her death I got a call from Andrew, Jack's second son. He had more shocking news. Jack had suddenly started suffering breathing problems and headaches. Uncertain, the doctor sent him to a specialist, who immediately sent him for a brain scan to confirm his suspicions. The scan showed a tumour the size of a golf ball! Jack was told that he had a malignant brain tumour, which would require immediate surgery.

How was he going to handle this? He was a hyperactive man, both physically and mentally, who had little patience for illness with others let alone himself. By the time I got the call, he was already out of surgery and in ICU. Jack's world had crashed and I was very sad for him.

The next call was sombre and the prognosis for the future, poor. He must have been all over the place, trying to come to terms with the life changing horror in his head. He had so many plans for the immediate future, which now were not a priority. However, one development was in an advanced stage. He had purchased a beautiful plot of land on a south facing hill at the south western part of his beloved Tortola. From there he could look across the Sir Francis Drake Channel to Peter Island and St John Island. This was always planned as his own bolt hole and also a place to share with the love of his life and his family.

He now treasured the thought of going there at the earliest possible time. Of course, Jack now faced into long term treatment and suffering, but there would be gaps between and it would be then that he would flee to his haven and bathe his body in the life enhancing sun that he loved.

Chapter Forty

The Endgame
14th February 2010

It was morning when I awoke and it was my 72nd birthday. I lay on my bed on my own, no Lizzie beside me to hug and wish me a happy birthday. But then I had no reason to feel good because we were hit with another bit of shocking news. A phone call the night before last revealed that Lou was in hospital and diagnosed with cancer. Lizzie got the train to Dublin the next morning to go and see her and find out what she could. Poor little Lou, she didn't deserve this. Lulu, Steve and Joey were in Yorkshire for a few days and we decided not to tell her until she returns in a couple of days. She was always close to her Aunty Lou and would be distressed with this news.

I returned from a nice walk with Jet, Lulu's dog. He's a black mongrel, very like a border collie without any white. We went into the town and along the river for a bit. He has boundless energy and exercises me. Today I was on my own, however; Lizzie caught the ten o'clock train and hoped to be back in Cork by one to join me, Johnny and Gerit for lunch at our favourite restaurant, Eco's in Douglas. Johnny was very sad with the news of Lou and planned to go and see her in two days.

The next day, Lizzie and I were in the departures lounge waiting to board the Aer Lingus flight to Malaga. It appeared to be on time. After months of very cold weather, the sun beckoned and we hoped for temperatures of 15 degrees or higher. An hour later, we tucked into a hot breakfast and relaxed at 35,000 feet. About an hour afterwards, the captain announced that we were now over the northern coast of Spain, though unusually, we could see nothing below but solid cloud. Thirty minutes elapsed and nothing had changed. The time had come to start our descent and still there were solid clouds. In all the times we have made this trip, we had never seen all of Spain under cloud.

Soon the turbulence started. We continued our descent for 10 minutes with increased turbulence; there was no sign of the deck. Then at around 1,000 feet a small break reveals the land below. A sight of the coast. Jesus! The sea from the beach for about half a mile was brown! There were great lagoons of brown water inland, floods! All the while, we drop like a stone then buck upwards. The plane juddered and the wing was flexing alarmingly. Lizzie's hand and mine were locked in a nervous embrace. The clouds broke as we slashed into them, crazy colours reflecting the land below. We descended lurching and bucking.

Then at the last minute the engines roared to full power, we were forced into the seat, the nose of the plane eased us upwards again. Continuing skywards, it was a full five minutes before there was an announcement.

"Malaga tower has aborted our landing due to extreme weather. We have been diverted to Seville and will arrive there in twenty five minutes. Please remain seated and with your seat belts fastened."

Two hours later, we flew back to Malaga and the weather had improved, but was still rough. It was with much relief that we landed safely, picked up our hired car and drove the 300 kilometres to Vera. It was nearly midnight; we were five hours late and tired. Lizzie couldn't get Lou out of her mind and wished we didn't come. I managed to convince her it was the best thing to do and that we would spend plenty of time with her in a couple of weeks.

Lily and Bootsie arrived in a couple of days and the long range forecast looked good. We were looking forward to having some fun with them and showing them around this lovely place that we have made into a second home.

In the writing of this book, I have reached into the dim distant past and I am in awe at the capacity of memory to retain and recall these deep, ancient events.

The threads and strands of memory
Are often random and once started,
will stir the heart and mind.

Like a river, life has a beginning and end.
At ,birth, a baby is a blank canvas
Like a river on high at its headwaters.

The energy of childhood and youth
Are mirrored in the turbulence downhill.
Both capture and gather riches on the way.

Searching and finding, reaching and falling
Energising youthfulness, overcoming obstacles
Twisting and turning but laughing with joy.

Headlong rush of youth slows to the broader
Arena of maturity, but hold, challenges remain.
Other lives join and entwine, still learning.

Generation of new life and tributaries breathe
Zest and continuity through fortune and ill.
To prevail is to continue to new generations.

The soft broad meadows are the endgame,
Old age and the sea beckon, reach out
To achieve full cycle and leave a mark.

Wow!